Praise For Henry Wood

I am new to the Henry Wood Detective Agency world, but am glad I stumbled upon this little gem. Brian Meeks has successfully led us around and through the world of Henry Wood, Luna Alexander, Sylvia Culberson, their respective families, and their friends. An added bonus is the as-yet unsolved mystery of the secret (or, not-so-secret, now!) closet and its gifts from the future. While every mystery has a few "obvious" moments, this particular mystery manages to keep us on our toes as we delve further into the pages to discover the secret behind the missing fathers. Meeks doesn't give all of Henry's secrets away immediately; he allows a few things to be played close to the vest. The best part is the promise of "more," as we know Luna and Henry may reconnect, the closet needs to be investigated more, and Mike and Francis are BOUND to lead us into a mystery or two of their own. Henry Wood Detective Agency receives a definite thumbs up!

~ Angeles Winesett

Private detective agent Henry Wood is a man who plays by his own rules, cunning and assiduous he'll stumble across one case that isn't all what it seems. It's January 1, 1955 when a striking dame named Luna Alexander guided by her father's wisdom falls upon Henry Wood's office; an investigator trained more in the ways of small time crimes and petty fall outs must now unravel a mysterious case. In this game of betrayer and the betrayed Wood determined to bring about justice to his client faces danger with a witty quip and willingness to risk anything for the sake of lawfulness. This is a great book that keeps you guessing the plot *ending until the very last page, will it play put as you suspected? Great read!*

-Cassie Olivia

I felt I'd entered Ali Baba's cave when I came across Henry Wood Detective Agency. Brian's masterful way of telling stories within stories conjured up images of the old TV series "Moonlighting," perfectly evoking an alternate universe where bad stuff happens yet good guys win, in the classiest way possible.

-Shonali Burke

Henry Wood

Detective Agency

Brian D. Meeks

HENRY WOOD

DETECTIVE AGENCY

All Rights Reserved
Published By
Positive Imaging, LLC
9016 Palace Parkway
Austin, TX 78748
http://positive-imaging.com
bill@positive-imaging.com

Contents

ONE

Shades Of Grey

It isn't the weather, or the city, or the cars passing that strike Henry. It is how, at 3 am, everything seems so black and white. It is 1955. His life is going to change and there will forever be shades of grey.

The city seems disinterested in the goings on of a single detective, wandering home after ringing in the New Year. All around there are people out, smiling, kissing, and more than a few stumbling. It is two more blocks until he reaches his apartment, alone. He has a house, but doesn't want to drive, which is why he keeps the tiny apartment. It is nice to be able to stay in the city if the need arises...or the drinks are flowing.

The life of a private detective isn't so glamorous. Most days are spent chasing deadbeats, or watching cheaters, or just sitting alone in an office wondering how one ended up here. Henry got to his place, and stumbled through the front door-not quite hitting the floor, but needing to put a hand down. He was several sheets to the wind and couldn't remember the blonde's name. The one at the bar, with the great smile and huge...

He tossed his hat in the direction of-but nowhere close to-the hat tree. He staggered to the kitchen table. There was a bottle of vodka sitting there, waiting for him. Being a thinker, Henry had placed it there before heading out to celebrate the New Year, knowing it would welcome him home if he made it back in one piece. He had forgotten a glass, so he took a small pull from the bottle. The warm glow of a New Year and the thought of the blonde's midnight kiss made him smile. He just wished he knew her name or where she had gone.

Some detective, he thought to himself. You can't even keep track of a dame you are kissing. It might have been the sailor at the end of the bar. He had been giving her looks. Case closed, he thought to himself. Not because he was sure, but because he didn't care. He decided he should go to bed, but while he was getting up the energy to go to the bedroom, passed out at the table.

In a flat in Brooklyn, a dark haired woman sat alone. She couldn't believe it. Her frantic worrying and pacing hadn't helped, so she tried several hours of tears, to no avail. Now she just sat in her kitchen, legs pulled up to her chest, alone with her fears. She looked at the clock; it was 3:37 am.

On the table next to a plate of fresh baked cookies, was a pad with an address on it. The name of the detective she had found in the phone book was underlined 3 times. She had planned to go visit him on the 3rd, which would be Monday, but the anguish had become unbearable. She decided she could go into the city in a few hours and leave a note for him. It wouldn't really speed things up, but she needed to do something. She was very tired and ended up writing the note and going to bed. "Dear Henry," was as far as she got before her head was resting by the cookies.

TWO

The Client

Henry's head was still throbbing from ringing in the New Year. He looked at his calendar, a present from his brother in Manhattan, a New York Giants fan of all things. The calendar had a team picture of The World Series Champion Giants, who swept the Cleveland Indians in 4 games. It was galling for him to look at, and he mumbled to himself, "At least the damn Yankees didn't win their 6th in a row." Though Henry didn't care for the Giants, the previous two years had seen his beloved Brooklyn Dodgers beaten by the Yankees, and he could barely stand it. But looking at Jan 1, 1955 filled him with hope and optimism. This would be the year for Robinson, Hodges, Snider, Reese, Koufax, Newcomb, Campanella and the boys. His daydreams were interrupted when there was a mouse like knock at the door. He started to yell, "Come in", but then lowered his voice and mumbled, "Yes?" His headache made him wince in pain.

The door opened slowly, and a tall svelte woman eased herself into his office. Her dark hair was pulled back in a bun. She was really quite striking, but obviously shy. He guessed librarian. "May I help you?" he asked, trying not to sound miserable..

"Are you Henry Wood, the detective?"

"Yes, and you are?"

"I am Luna Alexander, and I am afraid my father has gotten into a sticky situation. I need your help. I am sorry to bother you, and I didn't think you would be here, but…"

Henry was a detective by day and a woodworker by night. To be truthful, he was a moderately good sleuth, but a subpar craftsman. Just two days earlier he had been gluing up a jig for his router, to cut perfect dados, and the squeeze out had gotten everywhere. It had been a sticky situation, in its own right. He turned his attention back to Luna, who, he was sure, wouldn't be interested in his gluing issues.

After she had told him about her father, his background, and the last time he had been seen, Luna asked if she might sit down. When she took a seat, it seemed as if the weight of the world was threatening to crush her. Her look was defeated and sad. "Will you help me?"

Henry was about to say it sounded like a missing persons matter for the police, but instead said, "I would be happy to take your case, Luna." She gave the slightest smile, stood and shook his hand. Henry wasn't sure, but he thought he caught a glint of hope in her eyes. She handed him an envelope and said, "My address and number are in there, along with the retainer. Please let me know as soon as you find out anything."

As the door closed, he took out his little notebook and jotted down the details. He is a senior-level accountant with the Smith, Havershome and Blickstein law firm, and has been with them for 20 years. Lately he had seemed distracted. He and Luna lived in a modest flat in Brooklyn and he took the train into the city. Luna worked at a bakery and was up and gone before her father, but also arrived home several hours before him. She described him as a meticulous man. He liked routine and always came home at 6:22 each evening. Lately however, he had been getting home at all sorts of odd hours and would skip dinner, not even bothering to listen to the radio. He loved his job, he loved radio mysteries, and he loved routine. She mentioned first noticing something strange when her father didn't even react to 'The Shadow' going off the air.

Henry wondered if 'The Shadow' knew what lurked in the heart of Mr. Alexander. He headed back to his tiny little house and into the basement. He checked his magic closet, which had a time portal to the future. The story of the portal was a mystery Henry had not been able to solve, but since it hadn't sucked him into an abyss, and often gave him presents, he didn't care. Occasionally a new and wonderful tool would show up. The Bosch router had arrived just a month or so earlier with a magazine describing all sorts of things it could do. Today it was empty. The glue up from the day before was ready for him to start the next step. He found woodworking helped him mull over his cases.

The instructions in the magazine indicated the dimensions are rough. Henry figured he needed the practice, so he devoted considerable time to precision. After cutting two pieces, he realized he hadn't accounted for the thickness of his circular saw blade and had also made a measuring error of two full inches. It amused him that his attempts at precision had been such an abysmal failure. Henry had anticipated as much and had purchased plenty of extra lumber in preparation. On the upside, he had gotten much more comfortable with his circular saw. Henry was a glass half full sort of guy.

He took a few photos of the glue up and went upstairs to call Mr. Alexander's firm. Then his foggy brain remembered it was Saturday and also January 1, so he would have to wait until Monday. He returned to his jig and thought about Luna.

THREE

Monday Morning

Sunday had been relaxing. Henry spent the day finishing the dado jig for his router. He was starting to get comfortable using the router and was able to create a straight edge and from that square up the jig. He could hardly believe it when he put the square on each corner, and they were all at 90 degrees. What a rush. After he finished the jig and photographed it for posterity, he relaxed a bit and started a new case journal. He jotted down a few of his thoughts.

Jan 2, 1955, A New Year…A New Case. 37th floor, Chrysler Building, Office 16…Go there in person, meet Mr. Alexander's co-workers, look for clues. 8 am Monday.

Henry had called Luna, just to check if she had heard from her father and told her he intended to look around his office on Monday. She mentioned she suspected someone at the firm. Her father had been missing since Dec 24th, and Monday would be the first day the firm was open since he disappeared. Henry wondered if they knew he was missing. He would need to be coy.

The door of Mr. Alexander's office was mahogany and had his name on it. He walked in, and a weathered woman, with a serious look, was sitting behind a desk. She had a slight scowl on her face and was opening the morning mail. She looked up and asked, "May I help you?" in a voice that was much kinder than Henry expected. "Yes, I was wondering if I might speak with Mr. Alexander," he said, taking off his hat. He had decided to play it cool and gauge her reaction.

"Mr. Alexander isn't in yet, but he should be here shortly, he is never late. Do you have an appointment?" she said, while continuing to open letters.

"No, I was hoping he might have a few minutes," Henry said; sure now she wasn't aware he wouldn't be coming in.

She opened another envelope, and the phone rang, she answered and then said, "Excuse me, but are you Mr. Wood?"

"Yes." This caught Henry off guard, but he was clever enough to put on his nonchalant expression. He assumed she would elaborate. He was correct.

"Mr. Alexander apologizes for being late; you may wait in his office. He will do his best to get here as quickly as he can." She hit a button under her desk. There was a low buzzing sound and she stood up opening the door and showed Henry inside.

The office was nicely decorated. There was a large art deco desk and bookshelves along both walls. Henry noticed two plants, of equal height, in each corner behind the desk; in fact, everything was exactly where one would expect it to be. Luna had described her father as meticulous, and now that Henry saw where he worked, he understood. The desk was free of clutter, save for the new pad of paper by the telephone. The phone was placed so it was parallel to the edge of the desk, with the cord draped neatly over the side. Next to the pad was a group of 6 pencils, which were all lined up next to one another. They all looked to be the same length, and as Henry looked closer, he noticed something odd. Every pencil was rotated so the brand name was not showing, except one. Henry looked around the office and didn't see anything out of place. (not in book)

Having spent his entire Sunday fastidiously measuring and re-measuring every single cut and drill hole, he was feeling like he understood what it was like to be so precise. Though he wasn't normally a neat and organized person, he appreciated its advantages and the esthetic. Leaning forward he carefully rotated the pencil. On the other side was a set of six numbers. He read the numbers to himself, 1, 2, 3, 5, 7, and 23. He put the pencil in his pocket and pushed the other ones together. Just then, he heard the buzz of the door. He quickly sat back down.

The secretary walked in and said, "Mr. Alexander just called and he is sorry, but he is not going to be able to make it into the office. He asked me to apologize for not being able to discuss your numbers."

"Thank you" Henry said, as he stood up to leave.

"Do you mind me asking; are you a client of the firm? I thought I knew all the clients."

Henry, quick on his feet, said, "I am considering this firm. I met Mr. Alexander recently, and he offered to go over my books. He said that each partner has different strengths, and he would advise me which one might be best. I won't give my business to just any firm."

This seemed to satisfy her, and she smiled.

While he rode the subway back home, he thought about the numbers. What did they mean? Obviously Mr. Alexander is still alive and well, but what is he up to. How did he know I would be there at 8 am? How could he have known I would find the numbers? Henry had gone into the city looking for answers and only found questions. The detective, in him, decided he needed to think, which he did best while tidying up his workshop. Mr. Alexander's office had rubbed off on him. He could clean and think. Plus he needed to find a place of honor to store his dado routing jig.

FOUR

A Good Review

A rotund man sits at a typewriter, his sausage fingers dance over the old Underwood. He puts down his thoughts, his gospel if you will. He is revered or feared by all. There isn't a middle ground. He is the restaurant critic for the Brooklyn Daily News. If he likes a new restaurant then it will become an instant success. If he unsheathes his poison pen then the restaurant owners will be spending their days in the serving line of the local soup kitchen.

The clicking of key strikes is like a symphony to Francis Le Mangez. Today he is happy and full. "The soup was a delight and made me want to weep with joy. The Singe Café's famous monkey flambé, in a white wine sauce, tasted as if angels had prepared it, and I savored each bite. If you go out for monkey only once this year, make it the 'Singe Café'."

Francis had an office across from The Henry Wood Detective Agency. Henry likes Francis and they occasionally discuss food, politics and baseball, while throwing back highballs at the bar on the corner. Francis is a food snob, but he also appreciates a greasy burger and a beer. As Henry put the key in his office door, Francis popped his head out, and said, "Your cop friend was here looking for you. I took a message."

"Really? What did he want?"

"Tell Henry to call me as soon as he gets back," said Francis, as he handed the tiny piece of paper to Henry, with a pretentious scowl. Francis and Mike McDermott didn't get along.

"Thanks", said Henry, "Eat anything good lately?"

"I had a wonderful dinner at The Singe Café on 17th Street last night. I am writing it up now," he said, and turned around disappearing into his office.

Henry walked into the Wood Detective agency and put his hat on the hook by the door. He took off his overcoat, and hung it next to the hat. Sitting behind his desk, he put his feet up and looked at the pencil. The numbers, so neatly written, were a message. He felt it was a message specifically for him, but he didn't know what it was, or what he was supposed to do with it.

Henry picked up the phone and called Mike. Mike McDermott had been in law enforcement for as long as Henry could remember. He solved more cases than anyone in the 5 boroughs, by using his razor sharp analytical mind and sometimes a massive right hook. Mike loved chess and music. He owned every bit of vinyl by Enrico Caruso. He also enjoyed gardening and had an encyclopedic knowledge of root vegetables. When he was young, his nickname was 'Yam'. He was called 'Yam' until a couple of fights and a growth spurt between 9th and 10th grade. After that he was called 'Big Mike'. Henry just called him Mike. Mike McDermott didn't have any use for private dicks, but he liked Henry.

The phone rang once and the voice on the other end bellowed, "Mike here...go."

"Mike, I heard you were looking for me."

"So, Frenchy gave you my message. I'm surprised."

"He isn't so bad, sort of an acquired taste."

A grunt came over the line and Mike continued, "Word on the street is that you're poking around the Smith, Havershome and Blickstein law firm."

"So what if I am?" Henry played it cool. He didn't want to tip his hand. He actually didn't even know which cards he was holding, but he figured if Big Mike had gotten wind, then something must be up.

"Listen Wood, this is serious business you are sticking your nose into. If you know anything, you best come clean, before you get hurt," Mike said, trying to be intimidating. He didn't have to try very hard.

"You threatening me, Mike?"

"Not me, but there are some dangerous people involved. I'm trying to look after you," he said, as his tone softened.

"Dangerous people eh?" Henry said, trying to sound confident and hoping Mike would give him a clue as to what was going on. Henry needed a clue.

"I'm talking about the Italians. The word is some accountant has gone missing and they're anxious to find him. He knows things, things that could make a lot of people unhappy."

"Thanks for the heads up. I will try to keep my head down," Henry said, and hung up the phone.

Mike made a good point. Henry made his living battling unfaithful husbands, not angry gangsters. He wondered if he was getting in over his head. It didn't matter though, he had given his word, and he was going to follow through.

Henry was unsure of his next move and decided to head home. When he checked his magic closet he found there was another gift from the future. A plastic case with a silver disk in it and a thing called a DVD player with a tiny screen that looked sort of like a television. The DVD was entitled simply, "Tage Frid", and it appeared it had come from 1997, as that was the copyright date on the back. Henry was pleased with his gift from the mysterious closet, and when the screen came to life, he marveled at the picture. It was in color.

Tage Frid came from Denmark in 1948, "after a couple of thousand students, I learned a few things," said the voice from the tiny speakers, and after 75 minutes he had witnessed the charming old man teach him how he cuts dovetails, fixes a mistake, builds a drawer for a perfect fit, glues up pieces and discuss his thought process in design. Tage Frid puts to use a jig he built 30 years ago, in the video. This part showed him how important details were to the old woodworker. Henry quite liked the Danish woodworker's style. He thought about the DVD. It was made 40 years in the future, about a man who was old, but today, in 1955, Tage Frid is a young man, who just arrived in the US a few years ago. Henry watched the DVD twice and marveled at the beauty of his furniture. He wondered if the closet would send him more of these DVDs, as they were very entertaining. He wished he could show someone his new toy, but he never told anyone about the time portal in his closet, for he feared that if he did, it just might disappear.

He tried to imagine what Francis would say, what sort of review he would give this Tage Frid show. Henry knew that his recommendation would be an A +. He carefully put the DVD back in its case and put it and the player in a drawer under a blanket. He went to bed, thinking about Tage Frid furniture, and thinking about the numbers, 1, 2, 3, 5, 7, and 23.

FIVE

Degenerate Gambler

Jerry McMurry stood five feet eight inches, weighed a buck twenty, and had two miserable kids with an awful wife. He liked to gamble. It was hard to tell if he lost more at the track, or at life, but which ever was worse, it was clear he never caught a break. Nor did he really deserve one.

Tommy 'The Knife' made a point of knowing the particulars of his customers. A little bit of knowledge helped persuasion go more smoothly. Many a man would take a beating, but crumble at the thought of something happening to the wife and kids. Tommy was different than the other bosses, as he wouldn't hesitate to kill a guy's wife, just to make a point. To the other families, this meant he lacked honor. Honor is everything.

The problem today though, Tommy was sure that threatening Jerry's family would be pointless. He could kill them, but he didn't think Jerry would care. It might even be doing him a favor. He flashed a cold smile at Jerry.

"I'm gonna pay Tommy, I just need a little more time."

"Where you gonna find fifteen large?"

"I'll get it. Just give me a few more weeks."

"Jerry, you are a stupid mic and a degenerate gambler. You couldn't pick a trifecta box in a three horse race. Furthermore…"

Screaming, "Don't interrupt!", then calm again, "I would normally explain to you, the terrible accident which might befall your family, but I have seen your family, and I don't feel like doing you any favors."

Jerry shrugged.

A couple of very large guys standing by the door laughed. Tommy smiled at their chuckles.

"This guy," pointing at Jerry, "The only thing Jerry is worse at picking, than horses, is broads."

They all roared. The phone rang, and Tommy listened briefly, then gave a short list of instructions and hung up.

Jerry was beginning to shake.

"See the problem is that I know you can't pay. In fact, the whole world knows you can't pay. You might even take off and I would have to hunt you down like the dog you are. My first inclination is to dump you in the East River, and be done with it."

"Come on Tommy, we known each other since the neighborhood." Pleading.

"You were a punk back then, you still are…Now you made me lose my train of thought…"

"Boss, youz was saying we should dump his no good, broke, loser ass in the East River."

"Ah yes, that was it. I like the idea. I like it a lot. But I am a businessman and if you dead, you're no good to me.

Jerry sensing a break, "Thanks, Tommy, I just need a little longer to get straight."

Tommy walked around Jerry and patted him on the shoulder. "What we are going to do is work out a little advertising campaign. The best part, is you is da star."

Jerry looking a little worried. He may have been dumb, but he wasn't stupid. He knew this wasn't good news.

Tommy waving his hand at the two thugs by the door, "My business associates are going to fix you up with some bruises and broken bones. Then they gonna take you down to Aqueduct and leave you off to spread the word about what happens if you don't pay." The thugs cracked their knuckles.

Jerry was white as a sheet as the two men placed their hands on his shoulders.

"There is good news Jerry, while you are in the hospital, I am going to wave the vig."

One thug, "That is very generous of the boss, isn't it Jerry," he says, and then smacks Jerry in the head. "He must really like you."

Tommy, "Now that you mention it, I don't like him. The vig stands. That is $3000 per week, plus the $15,000. Now get this piece of shit out of here, he is starting to stink up the place."

Over the next two hours, Jerry, who was not religious at all, prayed for death. Tommy's men were professionals though, and they simply broke bones, and pounded his face until one eye was swollen shut, and the other was nearly closed. They dumped him in the parking lot, just as the crowd was coming out after the last race. The regulars, who knew Jerry, barely recognized him. Somebody called an ambulance and the word spread quickly.

Six

Tuesday

The next day, Henry arrived, at his office, bright and early. Francis wasn't in yet, as he preferred to roll out of bed at the crack of noon. It was quiet and Henry took out the pencil and a pad of paper. He looked at the numbers again, and then used the pencil to write down 1, 2, 3, 5, 7, and 23. Adding the numbers up, they equaled 41. Next he assigned each number a letter, a, b, c, e, g, y. Leaning back he pondered his first two attempts, scratched his head and dismissed them.

Twenty minutes and three more dismissed theories later, the sound of heels on the hardwood hallway floor caught Henry's attention. He was a bit of an expert on the gait of people. He could tell when it was Francis, he could tell when Big Mike was coming, and he knew that a woman who strode with confidence, was about to enter his office. The door opened. She stood there momentarily, as if to say, 'I am here, take me in, I am marvelous'. Wearing a Dior dress she had a figure that made an hourglass self-conscious and she knew it. The woman walked in and set her tiny purse on the corner of the desk and asked, "Are you Henry Wood?" in a voice that was dark and hypnotic.

With a nod Henry motioned to the chair. She sat down and crossed her legs. Boy could she cross a leg. Henry got up and checked the thermostat. "It seems you have me at a disadvantage?"

"I am Miss Culberson. I need your help and your discretion."

"What exactly do you need help with?"

"My father recently passed away," she said, adding a pause for a respectful sigh.

"I am sorry," Henry said.

"It is ok; it has been a month now. I have grown accustomed to the emptiness of the house. The reason I need your help is there are some issues with the estate."

"Issues?" Henry said with the voice he reserved for those occasions when he knew he was being fed a line, but didn't want the feeder to know. It was slightly lower with just a smidgeon of empathy.

"Mr. Wood, my father may have occasionally been creative with his books, but he was a good man. There is a man at the law firm we use, who seems to have it out for my father and now me."

"Which firm is that?"

"Smith, Havershome and Blickstein law firm here in town, and the man is Mr. Alexander. I think he is an accountant or something," she said, with a casualness that was a bit too casual. Henry considered taking offense at her remark about Manhattan being 'in town', as if Brooklyn wasn't, but her legs were really well crossed.

"Why do you think he is out to get you?" Henry asked, while trying not to look at her legs and intrigued that yet another person is looking for Mr. Alexander.

"He has been keeping a journal."

"An accounting journal, being kept by an accountant seems pretty standard, wouldn't you say?" Henry said, hoping to pry something out of her.

"I believe he had found some irregularities in my father's books, some tiny little omissions, and he wants to ruin my father's good name and me in the process," she said with another, albeit sadder, sigh. Apparently the thought of losing her inheritance was worse than losing her father.

"Why don't you just go to the partners and ask them to straighten him out? Surely, they wouldn't want to lose you as a client," Henry asked, knowing she would have a polished and prepared answer, but he liked to hear her talk.

"They don't know where he is. It seems he didn't show up for work yesterday. I need you to find him and get that journal!" she said, with an air of entitlement.

"What makes you think I can find him?"

"I have been told you are looking for him already. I just ask that when you find him, you bring the journal to me. I will pay you five thousand dollars. Here is half now and half when you deliver," she said, and stood, handing Henry a plain envelope. As Henry looked through the envelope, she grabbed her purse and left.

Now he had one job, two clients, and six crazy numbers. The rest of the morning consisted of a trip to the diner for a cup of joe and lots of dead end ideas about the pencil clue. Shortly after noon, Francis was coming down the hall with his buddy Don, a photographer at the Brooklyn Daily News. Henry popped his head out and said, "Hello gents, any good news today?"

"Is there ever?" scoffed Don. He spent most nights prowling the streets looking for seedy scoops. Francis just shrugged, "Hey, let me ask you guys something," Henry said, nodding towards his office.

"Sure Ace, what is it?" Don usually called Henry and everyone else Ace, as it meant he never needed to remember names. He was really bad with names and faces, and geography too. In fact, he was really only good at photography.

Francis, Don and Henry filed back into the office, and Henry read off the numbers. Francis shrugged again. If he couldn't eat it, he just didn't care. Don said, "They are all prime numbers. Well, technically, one isn't a prime, but most people don't know that."

"I hadn't noticed," Henry said, giving Don a nod of appreciation.

Don looked at the pencil and mused, "I wonder why there are 4 missing primes?"

The confused look on Henry's face, told Don he should elaborate. "11, 13, 17 and 19, are between 7 and 23."

"There are 4 missing numbers..." Henry said, out loud, but mostly to himself. "I wonder..." and his voice trailed off.

Don and Francis could tell Henry's wheels were turning, so they headed across the hall. Henry needed some wood time, so he grabbed his overcoat and hat and headed home.

When he got there the closet was empty, as it was most days. He took a piece of oak and rubbed his hand over it. *What would this be good for?* Henry thought to himself. He grabbed a ruler and a non-clue pencil and made some marks. The wheels were still turning.

The little piece of wood seemed to want to be turned into a tool holding device. Henry wanted to use the rare earth magnets he had bought some time ago, so he decided he would combine them with the oak and hang it on the wall.

He carefully marked out the spots. He would use his Fostner bits, to drill out holes for the magnets. A quick practice hole in a piece of scrap, and he was ready. The seven holes drilled out easily. Henry screwed in a magnet holder and was inches from plopping in a magnet when he realized once it was in, he wouldn't be able to get it out. Those suckers really stick together and the screw would have been hidden under the magnet. It was almost a blunder, but his brain was thinking several steps ahead, just like Mr. Alexander seemed to be doing.

Henry sanded the board for an hour and now was deciding if he should stain it. He had some General Finishes Georgian Cherry Gel Stain that had mysteriously appeared in the closet. He wasn't sure exactly how to use it, so he decided to think about it for a day.

Sitting down at the kitchen table he began to ponder out loud, "Mr. Alexander knew I would go to his office. He knew I would notice the out of place pencil. He is a cautious and meticulous man. He wouldn't just write down the clue. He would hide the clue." Henry was now convinced the real clue was 11, 13, 17 and 19.

It was shocking how the number 17 seemed to burn like a red neon light in his brain. It was so intense he was sure that this prime was the key to the next clue. The fog was slowly clearing from his mind. He was suddenly overcome with hunger and left to find some dinner.

Seven

Wednesday

The day had been long, very long and tiring. Henry's flash of genius was looking more like a flash of imbecile. When the number 17 started to flash in his brain, he searched and searched for what it might mean. After a while, he had it. Francis was working on a story about a restaurant on 17th Street. Henry was sure the missing numbers were an address. A map, a list, and 12 hours driving around the 5 boroughs, had been less than fruitful. It seemed there would be another clue, something that wouldn't be obvious to most, but would jump out at him. Maybe he wasn't as clever as he thought.

Doubt had crept into the equation. A couple dozen stops and nothing, though he had found an address across from a great tool store, so it wasn't a total loss. He popped in and there were a bunch of guys watching a demo of jigs and accessories for making woodworking easier. His favorite was a clever device which would aid in making wooden hinges. Henry knew he shouldn't stay too long, noted the address so he could find it again, and continued on his way. With only one address remaining, the possibility entered his mind that 11, 13, 17 and 19 may not have been the clue at all; maybe he should reconsider the original numbers.

His car rolled up outside 1113 West 17th, an apartment building in the warehouse district. There was a bit of a chill in the air. Henry walked up the steps and into the building. He glanced at the mailboxes. When his eyes landed on apartment 19, and he read the name, he almost stopped breathing, Tage Frid. Henry didn't have time to ponder the implications of his DVD from the future and his current case; he just knew coincidences, like this, were never coincidences. He stood, for a moment, outside apartment 19. He thought about the wonderful furniture created by this man. A deep breath, and then he knocked. No sound. He knocked again and nothing, not even a peep, so Henry slowly turned the knob. It was locked.

Henry looked around, nobody in the hall, so he quickly picked the lock. He leaned his head into the apartment and was both disappointed and sure he was in the right spot. When he saw the name on the box, he figured the real Tage Frid might be waiting to give him a message, or maybe Mr. Alexander was staying with him. What he found, instead, was an empty apartment. It wasn't just empty; the vastness of the 'empty' was stunning, and obviously the work of a meticulous man. Henry couldn't find as much as a speck of dust. He looked in the cabinets and they were bare.

Pacing back and forth didn't seem to help. It was getting dark, and Henry was tired. What was the clue? What did the emptiness mean? He took out the drawers in the kitchen. He looked behind the icebox. Henry even checked in the vents. *Focus*, he thought to himself. Henry walked to the window and looked out. Across the street was a warehouse. It did strike him as interesting that it was a furniture warehouse. He wondered what type of furniture they stored.

The street was empty. There were a few lights on in the warehouse, but it seemed, as if, most people had already left for the day. Henry tried to open the door; but it, too, was locked. Looking in the window, he could see a lot of furniture. Bedroom sets, kitchen tables, chairs, and lamps for as far as the eye could see. Henry's eye went to one piece. A cabinet, a Tage Frid cabinet, was sitting against the far wall. Henry decided, he had done enough breaking and entering for the day. Sometimes it is easier to just wait until regular business hours, than to be super sneaky, plus he was hungry.

He swung by Katz's deli on the way home and picked up a couple of sandwiches. Katz's is the oldest deli in NY, and had been slicing their own pastrami and corned beef since 1888. Henry loved Katz's.

After dinner he decided to give his magnetic tool holder a bit of color. This was his first attempt at staining anything. He sanded a practice piece of oak and tried it. Since there weren't any disasters, he grabbed the tool holder and went at it. Henry didn't have any idea about technique and simply lathered it on with the wooden paint stirrer. As soon as he had one side done, he wiped it off. It only took a few minutes to get the entire board covered. The gloves he wore were pretty messy and leaving marks, so he changed them for a new pair, and wiped every inch one more time, and then set it down to dry. It looked better than he had hoped. He preferred to take black and white shots, but he had a roll of Ektachrome and decided to go with color today. Henry liked to document his wood working triumphs. Tomorrow he would revisit the furniture store and try to figure out where to hang his new tool rack.

EIGHT

The Frid Cabinet

Henry woke up early and couldn't get back to sleep. The furniture warehouse didn't open until 8 am, but the clock said it was 3 am. He had been asleep for 4 hours. He lay there for another hour and decided he might as well get an early start. An egg sandwich, cup of joe at the diner, and some pleasant conversation with Mable, the sassy little waitress. An hour had passed. He rolled into the office at around 6:30 am and made a list.

Call Luna and ask if she has heard from her father and bring her up to date.

Call Miss Culberson and tell her as little as possible. Henry didn't trust her at all.

Buy groceries and some 1 x 2s in maple. Henry hadn't done any shopping in a while and his cupboards were looking as bare as 1113 17th Street.

And lastly and most importantly, check out the furniture warehouse and the Frid cabinet.

He tore the list off his pad and folded it neatly before putting it in his jacket pocket. Henry smiled at himself; he couldn't remember ever folding anything neatly. Mr. Alexander seemed to be rubbing off on him. He picked up the phone and 15 minutes later had updated Miss Alexander and reassured Miss Culberson that he was hot on the trail of a clue.

He walked down the stairs and out onto the street. His car was parked in the alley. The street was now busy with morning hustle and bustle. Henry could smell trouble at 100 paces. They sat in their car, reading the paper, but not turning the pages, just holding them. It was a dead giveaway. There was a third thug leaning against a lamppost, also not reading a newspaper. Henry decided they could tail him for a while. He would go poke around the lumberyard, buy what he needed and then lose them.

He found some nice hard maple 1 x 2's and picked up four 7 foot lengths, a bunch of screws, washers, and other miscellaneous items. He loved the lumberyard. It was a big place, almost maze-like. He knew everyone there and when he went up to the counter he whispered to the manager, "Hey Bill, could you put this stuff on my tab? I need to lose my friends. I will pick it up later." Then in a normal voice, "Oh wait, I forgot something." And he whirled around and headed back into the yard. The thugs followed, trying to look casual. Henry made a couple of quick turns and ran up the stairs and into the manager's office, which had a convenient back door. He winked at Bill's secretary, as he strolled past. She smiled. The thugs got back outside in time to see the taillights rounding the corner two blocks away.

Henry took a circuitous route to the furniture warehouse, just to be safe. After some words with the man in charge, he was allowed to take a look at the cabinet. He opened the cabinet it was empty. He looked into the drawers and admired the dovetail joints. Each drawer was carefully removed and each one was magnificent, but held no clues. The old man who had showed Henry to the chest asked what he was looking for, and Henry explained that he thought there might be a message from a friend. The old man wasn't one of those people who suffered from being curious and just shrugged.

"This cabinet does have a secret drawer." And he carefully showed Henry how it opened.

"That is incredible; I would have never found that," he said in awe.

"That is why it is called a 'secret drawer'," said the old man with a wink and a smile.

Henry pulled it open slowly and there it was, the journal that Miss Culberson was after.

"Would you look at that? It wasn't there before. I guess your friend did leave you a message."

"I guess he did," said Henry with a grin, a wink and a nod. He didn't open the journal past the first page; he saw the meticulous handwriting and knew that it was the work of Mr. Alexander. He just tucked it into his jacket and thanked the old man, slipping him a twenty, to forget that he had been there. Henry decided it wasn't safe to go back to his office, and he wasn't sure about the lumberyard, so he went to the library. He could bury himself in the stacks and give the journal the once over.

Henry took out his neatly folded list and turned it over, to use for taking notes. Page by page he slowly looked over all the entries. There weren't any names, and the numbers didn't make any sense at all. With each turn, he found page after page of neatly written and obviously coded financial data. When he turned the last page, there was a note, neatly taped onto the back of the last page.

Dear Henry,
You are as clever as I had hoped. It will soon be noticed that I am missing. I cannot tell you where I will be when you find this.

I myself don't know. I just know that the little book you are holding has all the financials to put a very powerful and dangerous man behind bars for the rest of his life.

I went to the police and told them everything just before Christmas. This was a mistake and I should have known better. It has gotten out that somebody at the firm was going to turn state's evidence. They didn't know who it was at first, but as soon as I don't show up for work, they will put two and two together. I gave Luna instructions to find you, if I ever stopped coming home. You need to make sure she is safe.

I can't come out of hiding to testify, as he has men everywhere. I need you to get this journal to the district attorney. After you do, I will need you to find the key, so that the book can be decoded. It is too risky to keep them together. Once the DA has both of them, he should have all he needs.

Thanks

A

Henry was suddenly worried about Luna. He hid the journal among the books at the library. He knew every floor and alcove of the library. The section on economic theory was generally ignored by the reading public, so he slid the journal behind several volumes by David Ricardo. He skipped lunch and drove straight out to see Luna. Henry worried the thugs he had shaken might have gone to find her next. He couldn't worry about the groceries, or lumber, or woodworking; he had to find Luna and get her to a safe place. He just hoped he wasn't too late.

NINE

Anthony Prepares For War

Anthony was born in Sicily and felt entitled. His father had grown up in the Bronx and made his mark during Prohibition. He was a well-liked family head. When Anthony's mom was pregnant with him, his father sent her back to Italy to have the child. It was important to them. When his father died of a massive coronary in 1949, Anthony took over the business. His entire life he had listened to his father's stories about how he had been cheated and should have been given Manhattan. He vowed to one day make it happen, for his father.

The rumors about a journal detailing all of Tommy's criminal enterprises had been a sign. It was his time. He called in all his boys.

It was cold and snowing. The doors to the shipping bay opened, and three more guys wearing dark overcoats and hats hustled inside. Everyone yelled to close the door. The center of the warehouse had been cleared out. There were chairs and a few tables. The cavernous building had all the windows blacked out, because Anthony used this for his 'secret' meetings.

He didn't have great management skills, but his men respected him. He wasn't especially tough. What he was good at was strategy. When Anthony decided it was time to move and sent the word out, he made sure that each man knew not to discuss the time or place. Keeping secrets, in their world, was no small feat. After many years of building his gang, he had instilled an almost military efficiency and chain of command. While other bosses would bark out a command, and then the worker bees would spread the word, with little regard for who might be listening, he had developed a fairly complicated group of signals.

Anthony got the idea while watching baseball. He loved the game, especially the NY Giants, though he would watch anybody. He never played as a child, and when he first went to a game, a young boy sitting next to him was listening to his father explain the signs the 3rd base coach was giving to the batter and base runner.. Anthony was fascinated. The father explained there was an indicator, which if not given, would mean all the other signs were bluffs to fool the other team. It might be a touch of the hat, or the elbow, or kicking at the dirt. It was hard to tell.

Anthony, who generally didn't like admitting he didn't know something, simply mentioned that it was his first time to a game. He wanted to hear more about the signals. The little boy became very excited. He started talking about the teams and players and added that catchers talk with the pitchers, using signs, too. Anthony was hooked. He bought everyone hot dogs and Cokes and enjoyed the rest of the game with his new friends. The Giants won 5-4 in 13 innings.

The next day he called a meeting with his top two guys. Two hours later they had a basic set of signs. When he brought in half a dozen of the guys, to tell them his new plan, one of them made a wisecrack.

He shot him in the face. The rest of the guys seemed more enthusiastic for his idea after that. In the years since, there had only been one breach of security. The guy who had talked about their signs was beaten almost to death, allowed to recover, and then beaten again. The second time he died. From that day forward there was order among the ranks.

Forty guys sat on chairs or crates. There were another dozen outside, looking for people who might be snooping around. The warehouse was cold; so four drums were being filled with broken pallets. Once the fires were lit, it warmed up considerably. Most of the guys were smoking and talking in small groups. Four others were standing behind a row of tables.

The tables were divided up, the first one containing pistols. Two guys were checking each one, cleaning them if needed and making sure they weren't traceable. The next two tables were for the machine guns, and the other two guys were going over each one meticulously. The last two tables were covered with ammunition, carefully labeled to indicate the caliber. Three guys who had just walked in stood by the burning barrel, quietly talking among themselves. "This looks serious, you see the tables?"

"Yeah, looks like we getting ready to hit the beaches."

"Who do ya think we going after?"

"I don't know, but I ain't ever seen so much iron."

"It must be big because..." His voice trailed off as Anthony and his two lieutenants entered through the back door. Everyone stood up, not at attention, but still respectful. Anthony hadn't insisted on such formality, but over time, they had started to take on the personality of a formal military. Anthony liked it.

"At ease everyone." Anthony walked around and greeted everyone by name. He asked a few about their wives and children, because showing interest is what a general did. The boys at the tables joined the others, and Anthony began to speak, "It is good to see you all." He paused, to smile at his troops. "I have told many of you, of the horrible treatment of my father. You know how he was wronged when Manhattan was given to that idiot and then again when Tommy was allowed to take over after his demise."

A few chuckled at the word demise, as everyone knew that Tommy had killed his boss. Anthony liked getting a laugh. "Tommy can't handle Manhattan; it is too much for his pea brain. If a man can't keep his business quiet, he don't deserve to be in charge. He don't deserve the rich rewards, which comes with such a valuable piece of real estate. His time has come. We gonna take Manhattan from him, and there ain't a damn thing he can do about it."

The cheers were more tepid than he had expected. The looks on the men's faces told the story. "Some of you may be worried about the size of his organization." He started to pace. "Ha, organization, I should have said disorganization."

A more rousing round of laughter followed, and Anthony knew he had them.

TEN

Frankie The Godfather

Frankie, sitting in his favorite leather chair, reading the paper, was just starting his day. His wife, of 45 years, still looked like the girl he had fallen for back in Sicily, though with grey hair. She sat sipping a cup of tea. Most of the day, the house would be filled with people coming and going, but from seven to nine, it was quiet.

The boss of bosses had rules and this one was sacred. Frankie had spent a lifetime building the trust and respect needed to run the five families. Though he could be ruthless, he was most known for his mind. He knew all the angels. In the last 30 years, since he became the top man, there had been a few challenges. Brash young men who thought bullets could solve any problem, learned, seconds before their own demise, brains beats brawn.

Frankie was also a firm believer in the theory of natural selection. There would always be rivalries between families; this couldn't be helped. Frankie let them fight among themselves. He considered himself the U.N., settling disputes only when they threatened world peace. If a man couldn't protect his family, he got what he deserved. It was the brash exuberance Tommy 'The Knife' had displayed, which caught Frankie's eye. He took him under his wing, and when the time was right, he gave him Manhattan. This was the most cherished borough, and the other families were understandably jealous.

Amata set down her tea, and said, "It seems Tommy is showing up in the news, almost daily."

Frankie folded his paper, a troubled look on his face. "He is. The volume is getting louder than I would like."

Frankie, though, at times he'd had a few broads on the side, loved and respected his wife. Over the last twenty years, he had been faithful, and they had grown very close. He trusted her and often used their golden two hours per day, to discuss his business. This was not how it was typically done; most of the wives were kept out of the business talk. There were very few people who knew how important Amata was to Frankie, or how much he valued her opinion.

"The sharks will start to circle, if he doesn't get things under control," Amata said, picking up a section of newspaper.

"It is the way of the Jungle. You are right though. It has been a long time coming; this will be a test for Tommy. If he survives, he will be formidable, might even come after this chair."

Shaking the paper open, "Oh, I don't know if he would go that far. He knows you made him."

"I said, he might try. I didn't say he would succeed. I have aces up my sleeve, he has never even heard of."

"I know you do dear. I like to think I am one of those aces."

Frankie stood up and gave his wife a kiss on the cheek. "You are my best ace."

The grandfather clock in the hall began to chime. The doors flew open, and a small pack of grandchildren stormed the castle of solitude. Frankie played with the kids until his first lieutenant Nicilo said he had a visitor.

Nicilo Bernini, who could trace his lineage back to Giovanni Lorenzo Bernini, had a strong jaw, was tall and lean. He spoke Italian perfectly, knew history, and respected the old ways. In 1946, Antonio Gecco, an eager up and comer, tried to make his bones by taking out Frankie at his favorite restaurant. Nicilo took two bullets, killed all three gunmen, and helped the restaurant owner's wife up off the floor. He never uttered a word of complaint about being shot. Frankie had pulled himself up off the floor and was looking around at his men lying dead. He wouldn't have noticed Nicilo, standing quietly in the corner bleeding, had it not been for the owner's wife giving a little yelp. Nicilo had been by Frankie's side ever since. Not only was Nicilo respected by Frankie, but he was genuinely liked and respected by all the families. He had earned his place.

Other than Amata, Nicilo was the only one who could tell Frankie he was wrong, and Frankie would listen. Of course, Nicilo never did it in front of others.

"Who do we have today?"

"It is Mr. Carlson, from the hardware store. It seems he has been getting some grief from some punks in the neighborhood."

They entered the study and Mr. Carlson was standing behind the two chairs in front of the desk. Frankie shook his hand, "Mr. Carlson, it is good to see you my friend. I understand there have been some problems."

"Yes, Godfather," he said, lowering his eyes.

"We will let them know to respect the valued members of the community, such as yourself and your lovely wife. How is Esther doing?"

"She is fine, thank you for asking. Thank you for helping me."

Frankie whispered something into Nicilo's ear. Mr. Carlson left and the rest of the day was spent solving other people's problems.

Eleven

Thursday Afternoon

The falling snow painted a layer of clean on the city. Henry didn't have time to take in the loveliness of it all. Despite being in a rush, he did notice the two children holding hands and spinning around, mouths open, laughing as they drank in the flakes. Their parents watched with pride. He assumed they were tourists from Florida; real New Yorkers just hunkered down and got on with their day.

Henry walked down the street towards his car. He had his eyes open for the thugs, though he couldn't imagine they would have guessed where he was heading. His pace was brisk, but not so much so that it looked out of place. It was still early enough that rush hour hadn't started, so Henry expected that he might be able to get out of the city without too much fuss. He was right. He headed north and ninety minutes later was pulling up the lane at the Alexander house. It was, a modest but elegant place, set back in the woods.

Henry's tracks were the only ones in the snow. He felt a bit better. All he knew for sure was that nobody had driven up the drive in the last hour or so. There didn't seem to be any lights on. He got out of the car, turned up his collar and with one hand on his hat, used the other to knock. He waited. No sound, no movement, just silence and the feeling of dread welling up deep inside of him. He knocked louder. When he began pounding his fists on the door, his mind was racing, and fear was replacing the dread.

There wasn't any sound, no wind, no storm, just the millions of flakes streaming down, narrowing the world to a space of about 20 feet. If it got any worse, Henry wouldn't even be able to see his car. He didn't know what he should do next. The barely audible creek of the door handle was deafening. Henry spun around to see the door open just enough for him to see two eyes peering out. As soon as Luna saw who it was, she flung the door open and yelped, "Henry." He was so relieved. She waved for him to come in, and as soon as he crossed the threshold, she threw her arms around him.

"Henry! I have been so alone and afraid. I'm glad you are here. Have you found Daddy?"

Henry returned the hug. He couldn't help but notice how warm she was, and how nice it felt to hold her. It was a good hug. "I haven't found him yet, but I have found another clue. I will tell you all about it. But right now we need to leave."

"In this storm?" she said, looking up at him. Her eyes were warm, but there was a bit of fear around the edges.

"Yes, I am afraid so. I have a house. Nobody knows about it. My neighbors don't know who I really am. It is a good place. You will be safe there.

"I feel safe with you." She hugged him again.

"Ok, now go pack a bag. Do it quickly, the storm is not going to let up, and we need to get on our way."

Henry locked the front door, mostly out of habit.

Henry watched her walk up the stairs. He stood in front of the fire to knock the chill off, while he tried to think one step ahead. It seemed like a run of good luck that nobody had gone after Luna yet. He wondered if they were on their way. He put out the fire after lighting a couple of candles. Luna had been napping on the couch. He folded the blanket and put it on the arm of the sofa. Henry walked to the front door and peered out the window. The car was barely visible. Luna was coming down the stairs when he saw the headlights. He stepped away from the window, and instinctively felt for the six shot cobra under his jacket. It was a bad time for a shoot out, as they would certainly have a lot more firepower. The car pulled up behind Henry's. Henry grinned and put the chain across the door.

He whispered to Luna, "There are some dangerous people outside. Soon they will be inside. We need another way out?"

"Who's out there?" She sounded frightened.

"I will tell you when we are safe. Now where are the doors?"

There was a pounding at the front door and someone was trying the handle.

"There is a back door to the patio, and the side door by the kitchen."

"Side door will do," Henry said, taking her by the hand.

It was dark inside; there were only the candles, which Henry had lit. The door erupted, as one of the thugs kicked it open. As soon as he heard the front door being kicked in, Henry opened the side door in the kitchen, and he and Luna ran out into the storm.

Inside the thugs were spreading out. One had run upstairs; the other was checking the cellar, while the third one was in the living room and heading towards the kitchen. Luna rushed to the passenger side and Henry stopped long enough to shoot out both the tires on the driver's side of the other car. He hopped into the car and fired it up. His car wasn't great in the snow, but it would do better than one with two flat tires. They were gone before the thugs made it back outside.

Over the next two hours, while the car crept back to Henry's place, he explained how he had found the journal and told her about the trouble her father was in at the firm. When they got home, Luna was tired and looked like she was about to drop. Henry grabbed her bag and showed her inside. A quick tour ended at the bedroom. Henry grabbed a blanket and pillow. He would sleep on the couch. Normally she would have objected, but she was too tired. Henry told her he would be downstairs if she needed anything.

Twenty minutes later Henry had pulled out some 1 x 2 maple he had lying around. He hadn't gotten back to the lumberyard, so he would just have to use some scraps to make something. He didn't care what he made; he just needed to create. He had seen an article by George Johnson of Canton, Oklahoma, where George had made a set of adjustable panel cauls. He measured each one carefully and then used his Japanese handsaw to cut them. The spacers for the cauls needed to be one and one half inches, and he needed 12 of them. The handsaw worked fine for those as well. He was rather happy with how good he was getting with hand tools.

Henry was extremely focused; he didn't even notice Luna sitting on the stairs watching. Her hair pulled back, she wore a big wool sweater and had her legs pulled up to her chest. She was a tiny ball of quiet, but she felt safe. Henry's precision and attention to detail reminded her of her father. She thought about him. She wondered where he was and if he was ok.

Henry finished the half of the first caul when he looked up and saw her sitting there. She was peeking out over her knees. He saw the corner of her eyes go up and he knew she was smiling. "Are you hungry?" he asked.

She nodded.

"Do you like Chinese?" He asked, walking around to the stairs.

"I love Chinese food, but can we get it, with the storm?" Luna said, poking her head up over her knees.

"Mr. Wong fears nothing! And it's only 2 blocks. So I think we are ok," Henry said, with a wink. Luna gave a little clap.

They ate and talked. Luna fell asleep on the couch; Henry pulled the blanket up over her shoulder and then got a blanket for himself. A few minutes later he was asleep in the chair next to the couch.

TWELVE

Bad News

The note simply said, "Went to the store for bacon, eggs, juice, and bread." Luna wiped the sleep out of her eyes and looked around. The house was small but cozy. She hadn't paid much attention the night before; she was too overwhelmed. On one of the walls were half a dozen photos of Washington DC. They were nicely framed and looked professional. The other walls were mostly covered by bookshelves. She ran her finger along the spines and read some of the titles, "Candide", "Fathers and Sons" a collection of short stories by Rudyard Kipling, a book of haiku, and various books about chess.

She went into the bathroom and splashed some water on her face. The sound of the front door startled her, but she immediately heard Henry calling out. Henry had also picked up the morning paper; the headline was disturbing, and he wasn't sure if she was ready. He hid it behind the credenza and headed into the kitchen. He heard the sink running in the bathroom, as he unpacked the groceries. Henry was an extraordinarily average cook; mostly he could keep himself alive. He could, however, make a good breakfast. He hoped she liked bacon and eggs. Then he thought to himself, *everyone likes bacon and eggs*.

Luna walked into the kitchen and said, "That smells delightful. Here, let me help." She took the spatula out of

Henry's hand. He wasn't used to being taken care of by a woman. It made him somewhat uncomfortable, but she looked really happy. He sat down at the kitchen table, trying not to think about the paper.

"Luna, you really don't need to do that, I can make breakfast," Henry said.

"You aren't used to being taken care of, are you?" Luna said with a little smile, and then continued, "Why haven't you found yourself a Mrs. Wood?"

Henry chuckled. He could tell she was feeling much better after a good night's sleep. He liked seeing her this way, though a subject change seemed to be in order. "So, how long have you been working at the bakery?"

Her eyes got big, "I love baking. Cooking is fun, but making cookies and cakes is the most wonderful thing in the world. I have been there for about 10 years. I make the best chocolate chip cookies in Brooklyn," she said, sticking out her chest as she pointed to herself with her thumb. "Since I came to see you, I haven't been in to work though. I have been too worried." Suddenly she was sad again.

Henry thought another subject change was in order. "What else do you like to do?"

She flipped the bacon over and cocked her head to the side, "I like books. I read all the time and not just for continued education. It helps me relax. I have a degree in literature from Oberlin College. Did you know that the first woman to ever attend college went to Oberlin?"

"I didn't know that."

"Her name was Lucy Stone and she graduated in 1847. I wrote a paper about her relationship with Susan B. Anthony. It got an A."

"I bet it did. Do you like to write?" Henry asked, seeing that her mood was on the upswing again.

Luna cracked an egg into the skillet. It didn't even look like she was thinking about it; she was a machine in the kitchen. Henry just sat and watched her precise movements; it must be an Alexander trait. Another egg hit the skillet with a sizzle, and she said, "I do like to write. I keep a journal and I write some stories, but I would never want to be a writer."

"Oh, why is that?"

"Because when you get done writing a story, you can't eat it," she said with a giggle.

Henry laughed too.

They sat at the table and ate breakfast, telling stories and laughing about Henry's college days. He had a thousand stories and she loved them. Her days at Oberlin were much tamer. Henry was exciting and he made her feel safe.

Henry mentioned that he was almost done with his cauls, and asked if she would like to come downstairs while he finished them. She said she would be down after the dishes. Henry tried to object, but she would have none of it, and sent him down to the basement to play.

When Luna came downstairs she sat next to the workbench and asked him about his project. Henry loved talking about woodworking, and wasn't ready to tell her about the headline.

"Cauls are helpful in gluing up boards. You apply the glue to the edges, lay some wax paper over both sides, clamp them lightly together, and then put a caul over each end," he said, while he sanded a small block of wood. "Once you tighten it down, they keep the boards from popping up when you tighten the clamps, and the wax paper keeps the glue from sticking to the caul."

"That is quite clever. I use wax paper for cooking," she said, and then asked, "How did you learn how to build a caul?"

"I read an article in a magazine. It described what I needed," he said, listing off the components. "8 pieces of 2 inch maple, cut to 36 inches long, twelve 2 inch by 3 inch spacer blocks, plus some 5 inch bolts and knobs."

"They look lovely."

"Thanks, the directions didn't call for it, but I spent a lot of time sanding each piece, so it feels nice and to avoid splinters."

The rest of the morning was spent talking in the basement. Henry wasn't aware that Mike was looking for him. He didn't know that his phone at his apartment in the city had been ringing off the hook. He knew nothing of the fire.

THIRTEEN

Luna

Luna missed her father dearly but felt much better being with Henry. She wondered about him. He was a bachelor through and through, but she sensed he enjoyed having some good cooking. She wondered if he had ever been in love. A couple of times she thought about asking but couldn't find the words.

It was nice watching him in the basement, working on his little projects. She liked a man who was good with his hands. The timer went off and she removed the cookies from the oven. It made her think about the bakery. She missed the early mornings, the baking, and especially the customers. Luna knew most of them by name, their kids' names, what their favorites were and who could be enticed to try something new.

Luna wanted to call the bakery and hear their voices, but Henry had told her it would be dangerous. She didn't understand what harm it would do, but she figured he had a good reason. She wondered what her father was doing. She imagined he was miserable, because hiding from the mob was not his usual routine. He hated his routine being changed. She sat down at the window and looked out on the gentle snow covering everything in a warm blanket. Luna wondered what type of woman Henry liked. She imagined he was partial to the movie star type, but she didn't know. It would be on her mind all day.

FOURTEEN

Salvatore Milano

Salvatore Milano was bigger than the other kids in the neighborhood. Teachers expected he would be slow, and he couldn't see an advantage in disappointing them. Easily bored, he usually had a book he could read while the teachers droned on. Sal was able to get passing marks with barely any effort at all.

There were a few guys he hung out with in his teens, but he didn't care for them much. They really were stupid. His real friends were his books. They taught him things, got him out of the city, and showed him the country of his parents. Each book held secrets, which they seemed happy to share, and they never judged him.

When high school was over he had two choices, join the army and maybe go to war overseas, or join a gang and fight in the wars at home. He chose home, as he didn't trust army food.

His first job, not surprisingly, was collections. People seemed eager to pay when he came a-calling. Salvatore instilled both fear and a sense of urgency in the debtors. It was lonely work. People who think you might break their legs don't line up to be buddies. It was much like his teen years, his peers - the other 'soldiers'- weren't very interesting to him. They all seemed to be interested only in chasing dames and getting drunk. They lacked imagination.

After fourteen months, he was given a driver, which meant he was to visit much bigger fish. His driver was an eager kid; not large enough to intimidate but could muster a fierce look. Sal thought he had potential. Joey was only a year younger than Sal, but the two were miles apart in size and experience. The kid was respectful, followed orders and looked up to Sal.

Salvatore didn't mind beating a man or killing him. He had a very clear picture of good and evil. Taking a baseball bat to the shins of a scum bag was fine. Roughing up a seventy-two year old grocery store owner, for weekly protection money, wasn't. Fortunately, the old ones didn't make trouble.

Kid, as Salvatore called him, was eager to learn the ropes. Most of the other guys would've told him to shut up and drive. Sal didn't see the advantage in keeping someone stupid. The more the kid knew, the better he could watch Sal's back. So one day he told him, "Most of the guys, they'd tell you to shut up and stop asking so many questions. They had to figure it out for themselves and are too lazy to help someone along. I think you have potential though."

"Really? Thanks," Joey said, trying not to sound too much like an eager puppy.

"You gotta understand something though..."

"Yeah?"

"This ain't a business where you advance by making waves. Sure there are guys with lots of flash who make it through the ranks. But for every one of them, there are a hundred who earn an early grave."

The kid nodded, pulling the car into a gas station and telling the attendant to fill it up.

"We gonna set up a few guidelines, you understand?"

"Sure, anything you say."

"I have some ideas about how to get things done. If I tell you something and you don't understand, you ask."

"I'll understand."

"If you don't, you ask, you know why?"

The kid was caught between wanting to act tough and needing to be truthful. "No." He looked ashamed.

"Listen Kid, this is what I am trying to get across, I don't expect you to know everything, there isn't any shame in asking. Or more accurately, there isn't any shame in asking me."

The kid smiled, "Thanks, Boss." It was the first time he used that moniker.

Salvatore smiled, "Best not call me that in front of the others. They might take offense."

The kid drove away and Salvatore continued, "The reason I want you to ask if you don't understand is that it saves time and headache. It can also save your life. A lot of guys get killed because they don't really know what is going on. It is the fault of their leader for not explaining the plan well enough and it is their fault for being too stupid to ask questions."

"Capice?"

"Got it."

"There is one more thing. I tell you something, anything, it is between you and me."

Joey nodded.

"You gonna talk about our business with your mom?"

"No."

"You gonna talk about our business with your dame?"

"No!"

"You gonna talk about our business with the cops?"
The kid gave him a dirty look and he laughed.

FIFTEEN

Paranoia

Tommy was superstitious, partly from his religious beliefs, but more from his own paranoia. He would see a black cat and then look for something bad to happen. When it did, it would confirm his belief in curses and bad luck. He combated his fear of bad luck by sticking to routines which didn't seem to bring it about. Of course, being a creature of habit isn't a good thing for a gangster, or anyone who makes a lot of enemies. Every other Tuesday he would go to Joe's Barber shop on 12th Avenue. Today he had sat in the chair, his face covered in a warm towel.

The man with the Tommy gun got out of a black sedan and looked around for the barber shop. It would have been easy to walk in and kill Tommy and his two men, had he not been driven to a pet shop with the same address, but on 12th Street. The shooter would have liked to pop the driver for getting it wrong, but he had a job to do. Twenty minutes later they had the correct address, but by the time they got there, an old man was sitting in the chair.

One might say it was Tommy's lucky day, were it not for the fact that he was known to have lunch at a small Italian restaurant, after every hair cut. Tommy, clean shaven, with perfect hair, sat with a couple of men and a friend who owned a car dealership. A bottle of red and a bottle of white wine were brought to the table, just as the shooting started.

Jake Holcomb, of Holcomb Cadillac, took three bullets with Tommy's name on them. It took but a second for Tommy to flip the table and find cover. He fired back, but it was too late. This is life in the jungle, as soon as there is a perceived weakness, the other predators strike. He was lucky to have a big friend dining with him. Tommy would have liked to blame a black cat or a broken mirror, but he knew it was the journal, which was the source of his curse.

Sal would think about the kid now and again. Kid was his first friend and, thus far, only one. It had been a few years, but he remembered the sound of Tommy guns cracking in harmony with the crescendo of breaking glass and two soprano waitresses hitting the high note called terror. The kid was hit five times and likely died before he hit the floor. A cost of doing business, Tommy had said. It left a bad taste in Sal's mouth.

He sat finishing his lunch. Three degenerate gamblers stopped in to drop off envelopes. The advertising had worked. Sal counted each envelope, carefully made a coded note on a piece of paper and dismissed them. When he finished lunch, his current driver took him to drop off the cash.

Sal walked into the office and heard Tommy screaming. The blond secretary, wearing a tight pink sweater, which accented her considerable secretarial skills, looked mortified. Tommy was prone to screaming, and she usually took it in stride. She could normally be found reading a magazine or doing her nails, today she just sat stone cold still. Sal saw her open her mouth, presumably to let him in on what was going on, but then she thought better of it. The sound of a bottle smashing against the wall said it all.

Sal had, quite on his own, started using a specific knock, long, short, short and then he would wait until Tommy told him to enter. It hadn't taken long before Tommy had started to recognize him and called him by name. Sal was a thinker and he imagined there might come a day, when in a rage, Tommy would shoot somebody through the door, expecting someone else. He was volatile like that. This is how Sal's brain worked, always planning, always asking 'what if'.

Sixteen

Tommy 'The Knife'

Henry took a couple of photos of the cauls and told Luna that he needed to head into his office and made her promise not to leave the house. She said she would read a book. Henry took the paper with him; he turned on the shower, and only then did he read the 'Big News'.

The headline read, 'Missing'.

An accountant with the prominent Manhattan law firm of Smith, Havershome and Blickstein is missing, and the police commissioner, Jonathan O'Rourke, has indicated that the entire department is scouring the city. Mr. Alexander is wanted in connection with the racketeering and money laundering case against infamous mobster Tommy 'The Knife'. It is believed that he may possess crucial evidence in the case, and the commissioner has asked the entire community to be on the lookout for the missing accountant.

The article went on to provide conjecture regarding the case, most of which wasn't at all accurate, but did fill out a fairly thin story. At least now, Henry knew which mobster was after Mr. Alexander. Tommy 'The Knife' was a ruthless thug who preferred to use a hunting knife to a gun. He had risen up through the ranks by collecting for the most powerful loan shark in the city and now ran a veritable army, made up of the dregs of society. Henry took a shower and shaved. He told Luna that he was off to the office and made her promise to stay inside, again. She agreed.

It was no longer snowing. The streets were wet, but traffic was light, as most had taken off work and stayed home. The drive was easy and Henry's thoughts turned to the case. What could be the next clue? He thought about the journal. He needed to get it to the DA, but first he wanted to go to the office and see if anyone had been around to see him. He needed to go meet Miss Culberson, as it appeared the journal didn't have anything to do with her father, and he wanted to find out who had put her up to hiring him.

Henry parked his car in the alley down the street from his building. He rounded the corner and immediately saw the crowd gathered around the front of the charred building that used to hold his office. He didn't stop to ask what had happened. He knew the answer. Henry went to his apartment, which was only 5 blocks away. He kept the apartment in the city as his official residence. Henry made sure that he spent at least one night a week in the place, just to keep up appearances.

Feeling the need for caution, he used the back entrance. There wasn't anyone around. The back stairs were empty, but Henry was extra careful. He listened for anything out of the ordinary. It was quiet, except for the baby crying in 5B. When he stepped onto the landing, nobody was waiting. Henry pressed his ear carefully against the door and there was only silence, not so much as a mouse in the house. It turned out that there weren't any mice, only rats. Henry opened the door and walked in. The door closed behind him.

"Mr. Wood, you owe me two tires," said a man, with a very thick neck, sitting in a chair in the middle of the room.

Before Henry could come up with a clever response, the man to his right, welcomed him with a sock to the gut.

"It seems you've been sticking your nose where it doesn't belong, Mr. Wood," said the man in the chair.

Henry was about to answer, when he got another greeting to the midsection.

"You tell your buddy 'Big' Mike that he messed with the wrong guy. If he wants a war then we will give him one."

The thug behind Henry brought something down on the back of Henry's head and he dropped to the floor. The knocking at the door caused Henry to come to. He moaned and said, "Come in."

Mike walked in as Henry was trying to sit up. He looked around the apartment. "They tossed your place pretty good, eh buddy?"

"I was thinking of having a decorator in anyway."

"I told you that they're some bad guys," said Mike, while helping his friend to his feet. "Maybe you best tell your buddy what you have been up to?"

Henry and Mike turned the kitchen table back upright and got a couple of chairs. He grabbed the bottle of bourbon from the counter and two glasses. "Was there anybody hurt in the fire?" Henry asked.

"No, it must have started around 3 am; we don't know the cause yet. You think it was your new friends?" Mike asked.

"I don't believe in coincidences." Henry threw back the shot.

"Now, what have you found out that has gotten Tommy's people on your back?" Mike asked, as he poured Henry another one.

Henry filled Mike in on the details, including the message they left for him. Mike promised to look into Miss Culberson for Henry. He told Mike about the journal and explained that he had it hidden and that they needed to get it to the DA. They each had another shot and sat without saying a word.

Seventeen

The Burnt Office

Mike spoke up first. "Hey buddy, I am going to need you to look around your office." Shrugging, he added, "Or what's left of it."

"I saw the fire, before I came up here to the welcome home party." Henry set the bottle by the sink and said, "Yes, I suppose we should go, let's get to it."

They took Mike's squad car and pulled up behind the fire chief's vehicle. There were still a few gawkers, gawking outside. The third floor windows of Henry's office were broken out and the bricks were charred half way up the 4th floor. It looks like the firefighters were able to stop the blaze from engulfing the entire building.

The chief gave a nod to Mike, "What brings you around Mike?"

"Hey Sparky, this is my pal Henry Wood," Mike said, and Henry stuck out his hand.

The fire chief and big Mike had been friends for a long time. Mike had given him the nick name 'Sparky' when he had emerged from his first fire, as sparks and flames gushed out behind him. The building was lost, the nick name stuck. "Good to meet you Henry, what can I do for you?"

Mike looked up at the building, "That 3rd floor office was Henry's; we wanted to take a look."

"It looks like the fire started in a trash can. The French guy called it in," Sparky said, motioning for Henry and Mike to follow him. Henry saw Francis, standing across the street with the onlookers, talking to a short round man with a small notebook. They walked up to the third floor and the chief explained that the fire had been contained to the one office, but the smoke had made quite a mess of the neighboring offices, including Francis's.

They trudged down the hallway and the rancid smell of smoke and wet filled the air. The chief said, "Now be careful, and don't touch anything, we are still investigating." Henry looked down at the floor, the glass from his door was in a couple of pieces with a couple of letters missing, "Henry Wood Detec e Ag n y." He stepped over the glass, careful not disturb anything, and into the office. The filing cabinets were opened and had been badly burned. The desk was mostly gone, as was his trash can. It did look like the fire must have started in the trash can and it also looked as if the offices had been given the once over, though it wasn't turned upside down like his apartment. Henry looked around for another minute and walked out.

Henry and Mike left the chief in the hallway, as he was talking to one of his men, and headed down to the street. Henry suggested they talk to Francis and see what he knew. He was still talking to the odd little man and when he saw Henry, said, "Henry it looks like we are going to have to move, my place is a mess too."

"You ok Francis?" Henry asked.

"Oui, I smelled the smoke, called the fired department and I got my butt outta there."

The little round man handed Henry a business card while saying, "I am Bobby Ward, and I am in the commercial real estate game. I have a place two blocks away, if you are interested. It is a great place and you could move in right away. I know you would love it." Henry took the card and said, "Thanks" hoping that would shut the little man up. It did not. "We could go now. I have the keys, we could go now, and you could check it out. Let's go, come on Mr. Wood, I know you will love it."

Henry put the card in his pocket, "Now listen Bobby, we are a little busy right now. I have your card, now scram." With that Bobby tipped his hat and said, as he scurried away, "I wrote the address of the building on the card, it is office 309, on the third floor, call me and we can see it anytime you like."

Henry, Mike and Francis talked for a while longer, and then parted company. Mike took Henry back to his car. He offered his couch to Henry, if he needed a place to stay. Henry declined, and said he would just get a room. He wanted to be alone. Henry assured Mike that the journal was safe and that they could get it tomorrow. Mike promised Henry he wouldn't mention the journal to anyone, though he was a bit offended, when Henry suggested there was a mole in the police department.

Henry drove back to the house, taking a long and cautious route. When he got home, the smell of chocolate chip cookies filled his nose. It was the first good thing that had happened all day. Luna yelled from the kitchen, "Henry, I did some baking. I hope you don't mind."

"Not at all, it smells wonderful. I will try one in a minute," he said, heading down to the basement. He went straight to the closet hoping he might find something new. He opened the door and there was a little grey box with the words Shop Fox on it. He opened it and there were 10 small brass bits of different sizes, two of them were marked 'locknut' while the others had different dimensions on them. He wasn't sure exactly what they were for, but he guessed they had something to do with his router. He put the little box with his router and went upstairs.

Eighteen

Sylvia and Winston

The silk sheets were divine but provided little comfort. Some days seemed to weigh more than others. Sylvia remained in bed despite Winston's repeated attempts to roust her. She thought about cotton sheets, day old bread, and her tiny room.

Sylvia felt sad, but not as much as she had before. Mostly she was confused about what was going to happen with her life. It all seemed like such a foggy mess. High society was not her world, though one couldn't tell it to look at her. She had poise and grace, she moved easily among the denizens of her new life. What she didn't have were close friends.

When she worked at the department store the other girls would invite her to go with them for drinks. She loved it. It was fun to gossip about who was dating whom and which one was going to land a husband first. It took only a couple of drinks before the real giggling would start. After that the talk was even better. A few of the ladies already had gotten their rings and delighted in giving advice. Mostly it was a bunch of tricks and wisdoms, which were sure to land a husband. They were the proof. These were the best times of her life and Sylvia missed them dearly.

The voice in her head said it was time to get up, or was it Winston again? She wasn't sure, but decided it was right. She swung her legs out of bed and eased her feet into the slippers. She put on her robe and sat down at the dressing table. The woman in the mirror drew the silver brush through her hair. Sylvia looked deep into the woman's eyes and saw her pain. She felt a deep sorrow for the lonely woman in there, just barely existing. The house was quiet, so quiet it almost made her crazy.

Another light knock at her door, "Miss Culberson, would you like some breakfast?"

"I am up now. Thanks, Winston."

"I am pleased to hear it. Shall I have something brought up?"

"No, I will be down in a few minutes. Some coffee and toast will be fine."

The staff consisted of two maids and Winston, a gentleman's gentleman. A house of this size would usually have a much larger staff, but Mr. Culberson wasn't quite comfortable with maids and servants, he was easing his way into the lifestyle. He always said he would hire more, once Sylvia got married and had kids. It was his dream to fill the house with grandchildren. Sylvia tried to talk her father into buying a smaller, more manageable house, but he wouldn't listen.

She walked down the hall past the seemingly endless rooms, some of which she had never been into. It seemed like such a waste of space. And that, too, made her sad.

NINETEEN

Winston

Winston was the son of a gentleman's gentleman, as was his father. Their family had been helping the rich and privileged appear better than they were, for centuries. His brother, had worked for a Lord in London, but passed away, a casualty of the German air raids during WWII. He wondered what he would think of his current employer. He imagined the advice would be to leave America and move back to London.

Winston removed two pieces of toast and spread butter and marmalade on each one; then set them on the table with a bowl of fresh fruit. The coffee was ready, so he poured her a cup, added two sugars and stirred.

The two maids were already tending to their duties, light as they might be, and so he sat in quiet contemplation. The recent events had been hard on Sylvia, as they would any person, but it was worse for him. He knew the secret and couldn't tell. He couldn't ease her suffering, and for that, he suffered right along with her.

She wasn't like other people he had worked for, not in the least, she was a proper lady. Sylvia was more proper than most of the terrible shrews who had 'breeding'. It came to her naturally. She was polite, clever and witty, even around the society folks who didn't deserve it. Winston knew it wasn't her choice, but she played the role with style.

He thought about the suitors who called and how she had run them all off since the explosion. He knew grieving, for he still felt the pain of the loss of his brother, but he didn't want to wall off the world, he wanted to let it in. Winston felt best around people. He liked it when Mr. Culberson brought over colleagues. It was a pleasure to serve them, to attend to their needs, and to see their appreciation. Mr. Culberson's friends were not high society folks either, though some were successful and had made their own fortunes. They all remembered life before, and never once looked down on Winston.

Winston thought about their late night conversations. How Mr. Culberson would stay up all night, working on a project, and Winston would sit and listen to him describe how it worked. Winston didn't know anything about science, or inventing, but still he was asked for an opinion. Often it was something simple, like, where would you put this handle, or if it could do this, would that be good. Winston would simply answer from the heart and explain why he agreed or disagreed with the idea. Often Mr. Culberson would look at him and say, "You know, I think you are right." Or, if there was a good reason, he would explain why Winston was mistaken. It wasn't the contribution, which was important to Winston; it was the joy in being respected. Mr. Culberson treated him like a friend, not a servant.

He heard footsteps and Sylvia walked into the kitchen. Normally the lady of the house would insist on eating in the dining room. Sylvia liked eating in the kitchen and reading the morning paper.

"Good morning, Winston."

"I wondered if you might miss it today."

"Yes, I wondered that too. But I am up. Life goes on and so must this day." She took a bite of toast and opened the paper with a crack. Winston noticed. She had not done that before. Usually she would take a section, lay it on the table, and then carefully turn each page. It was her father who snapped the paper open and devoured each story. Winston wondered if she even knew she had done it.

"Did you see this review by Le Mange? It looks like it might be a good place to dine."

"Shall I make a reservation for you, Miss?"

"A reservation for one? I don't think so. Maybe we could go together, it would be less lonely."

"That would hardly be proper, Miss. Perhaps one of the gentlemen callers, whom you have whooshed away, might be interested?"

"You think I should ask them out? That certainly wouldn't be proper."

"I could make a call and hint that..." There was someone at the door. Winston got up to answer it. Sylvia remained with her toast, but did seem a little bit surprised.

TWENTY

A Case of Déjà Vu

Henry's belly was full of eggs and bacon. His body ached from the encounter with Tommy 'The Knife's' worker bees. Several of his ribs could still feel their sting. He sat behind the wheel looking blankly down the street. Not a soul in site. All along the avenue were cars, some covered in snow, some cleaned off, but all of them resting and waiting for the day to begin. The sun was up, but the sky was too grey and depressing for anyone to know it. He pulled out and headed to see Miss Culberson.

He had talked to her on the phone with most of his 'updates' being a load of bull. Henry didn't believe she was on the up and up. Something about the way she dressed, which was intoxicating, and the way she described her father's death, just didn't ring true. He couldn't sense any grieving. Her line about worrying if her father's good name might be tarnished made him think she was hiding her real motive. Henry wanted to see her in her home. Read her on her turf. And maybe snoop around a bit.

He pulled into the drive. Opulence is usually wasted on Henry, but in this instance, he was impressed. He pulled his car up to the front door, parked behind the '34 Bentley 3.5 Darby. It was a black and cream colored beauty. He rapped the knocker against the massive door. Footsteps could be heard approaching and then a stately gentleman opened the door and invited him in.

"Good morning sir, are you expected?" the man said in a proper British accent.

"No, but I believe Miss Culberson will see me," Henry said politely. He watched him head up the massive front stairs. Henry thought about some of the great houses he had seen, Mansion House in London, The Breakers, and The Elms in Newport. This wasn't quite in their league, but not far off either. He guessed that it could be quite a while before she returned; depending upon which wing she was in. Henry loved art and immediately noticed the Hiram Powers' 'The Greek Slave' displayed prominently in the center of the entryway.

His feet echoed down the halls as he wondered around the corner. The hallway ran up to a set of giant mahogany doors. There were doors flanking the hall, each of them closed. Between each door there was a huge portrait. Normally one would expect to see family portraits, but Henry recognized two paintings by Thomas Gainsborough, the Lord and Lady of Dunstansville from the end of the 18th century. He was confident that they were not distant relatives of the Culbersons. When he spied the John Singer Sargent portrait of Madame Edouard Paileron, he knew that the Culbersons were new money, trying to buy their way into respectable society; and from the looks of it, doing a pretty good job.

The sound of distant feet approaching sent Henry back to his spot by the door. It was a good ten seconds before Miss Culberson appeared at the top of the steps. She flashed a big smile upon recognizing Henry, but quickly composed herself and replaced the smile with a more proper, albeit blank, expression. She seemed to float down the stairs. Each step was precise and refined, though it felt a bit forced.

"Good morning, Mr. Wood, how are you today?" She said.

"I am well, thank you," Henry said with an equally refined and overtly forced expression.

Seeing this, and knowing that he wasn't buying her routine, she relaxed a bit.

"Oh Henry, you see right through me," she said, while putting her arm through his and leading him down the hall towards the giant doors. "Now tell me, have you made any progress finding the journal?"

Henry wanted to get a read on her and she seemed to be relaxing, so he decided to see what he could learn. "I have been working your case, and yesterday, I got worked over by some of Tommy 'The Knife's men. You wouldn't know anything about that, would you?" he said, trying to push her buttons. He was surprised by her answer.

"No. Who is that?" She said innocently. So innocently, in fact, that Henry believed her. So he brushed off her question by saying, "Oh nobody really, just another interested party. I thought you might have heard your father speak about him."

"I didn't really know any of my father's friends. The only person who visited him regularly was that accountant Mr. Alexander. They would disappear into father's office and talk in hushed voices," she said, opening the giant doors.

The door led to a massive office, or was it a library, Henry wasn't sure. The desk in the center made him think office. She let go of his arm and said, "This is Daddy's office," in a voice that rang true for the first time since she had walked into his office.

"This is very impressive Miss Culberson." His eyes were scanning the walls, taking in as much as he could.

"Please Henry, call me Sylvia."

"Sylvia, how did your father die?" Henry said, trying not to sound insensitive.

"It was an explosion in his lab," she said, showing genuine remorse. Something Henry hadn't noticed in his office.

"His lab?" Henry asked.

"Yes he was an inventor. He had all sorts of patents. I can't even explain what all of his stuff does; I just know that he loved his work."

"You said that you suspected that he may have been cooking the books with Mr. Alexander, what makes you say that?"

"Look at this place," she said, waving her arms over her head slowly. Sylvia sat down in her father's desk chair and continued, "We moved here 3 years ago. Before that we lived in a small brownstone, and barely had enough to eat. I worked at a department store downtown. After mother died, he threw himself into his research and one day, he came home and said he had sold one of his patents. Two months later he sold another one, and then two more. It seems that companies were lining up at the door to get their hands on his inventions."

"So what makes you think he was up to something?"

"Well, he was so secretive, and two weeks before the explosion, he told me about the journal Mr. Alexander was keeping and that it could be dangerous for us. That is when he told me about you."

"Excuse me," Henry said, trying not to sound startled, though he clearly was taken aback.

"Yes, we had dinner, just like most nights, and then he brought me in here and told me about the journal saying that if anything happened to him, I should hire you to find the journal. He gave me your card."

She opened the top drawer on the right side and pulled out a business card. She handed it to Henry and said, "Oh and I had a bit of a hard time finding you, it must have your old address. I went there first and the office was empty, so I asked the bellman and he found out your current address for me."

Henry took the card and looked at it. He looked at it again. The address was not his, nor was it his previous address, as he had always been in the same building. He turned the card over and the back was blank. He thought to himself, *That is so odd, I have never had another office, but that address looks very familiar. This is just two blocks from my office.*

"What's wrong Henry, isn't that your card? You look like you have never seen it before."

"It does look like my card, but I have never..." He stopped mid sentence. He took out his wallet and removed Bobby's card. A chill ran up and down his spine. He slowly turned it over and read the back. The addresses were the same, right down to the office number, 309. Sylvia had just handed him a business card with, what appeared to be, his next address.

TWENTY ONE

The Lab

Sylvia looked at Henry, and cocked her head to the side. It was obvious to her that he was deep in thought. She didn't understand why he suddenly felt like he had to sit down.

"Are you ok? Would you like a drink?" she asked.

"I am fine, thank you, and yes please," Henry said, still looking at the back of Bobby's card and the business card that Sylvia had just handed him. He knew he didn't want to explain what he was thinking. The address would have seemed impossible, were it not for his closet, which he had grown to accept. He couldn't imagine being able to explain it to Sylvia.

The distinctive sound of ice cubes landing in fine crystal went unnoticed by Henry. Sylvia poured a scotch rocks; she hadn't asked what he wanted, because he looked lost in that place where her father went, just before his mind unraveled a mystery. She had seen it on her father's face many times, and knew that it was best not to break his train of thought. With the grace of a cat she set the drink on a coaster in front of Henry.

Henry was staring at the bookshelves behind the desk, but it looked like he was seeing past them, off to the horizon. Off to the ends of the earth for all she knew. A minute passed and slowly Henry reached out, slowly picked up the scotch, and took a sip. He didn't change his stare, but said, "Thanks, this is excellent."

Sylvia whispered, "You're welcome." She had returned to the desk and was watching him, completely intrigued by his motionlessness. It was as if she stared into his eyes hard enough, she might see what he was thinking.

The deafening silence was shattered when Henry asked, "May I see your father's lab?"

"Sure." Sylvia said, startled at the suddenness of his question. She stood up, grabbed her drink, and headed into the hall. Henry followed, taking sips of his drink as he walked. They crossed the entryway and headed down a hall that was the mirror image of the one they had just left. Henry was no longer paying attention to the art. Before they got to the end, Sylvia opened the last door on the left, and Henry followed her through.

The room was long and rectangular; they passed through it, to a door at the far end. This door led to a spiral staircase, which headed down. Though Henry was still deep in thought, he did notice that they seemed to be going down more than just one story. It felt like two or three. They had passed a small door and continued on until arriving at a heavy wooden door. Sylvia lifted the latch and pushed the door open. The hallway was entirely made of stone and felt like a dungeon, though it was lit with modern lighting. Henry felt he should be carrying a torch.

Sylvia paused by the door at the end of the hall. "I haven't been down here since the explosion. If you don't mind, I'll stay outside." She leaned down and pulled a flashlight out of a little wooden box sitting by the door. She handed it to Henry.

"I understand," he said, clicking on the light. Henry opened the door and walked into the lab. The odor of the fire lingered, but it wasn't the same as his office, it was more of a sulfur smell. The room was large and circular in shape, with a very high domed ceiling. It looked like there had been three workstations around a center area where there must have been something massive. All that remained now was a crater. The edges of the room had piles of equipment, glass and wood, which had been blasted out from the center. There were large bits of the ceiling on the floor. The basic structure still seemed sound, but the lab and its contents had been turned into a pile of rubble.

Henry walked all the way around the room. He didn't see anything helpful. Returning to Sylvia, he turned off the flashlight and put it back in the box. There was something he wanted to ask, but he wasn't sure how to broach the subject. He already knew that Sylvia wasn't tuned into her father's work, but he had a theory, a crazy theory, so he decided to ease into the question.

"Was your father alone when the accident happened?"

Sylvia said, "Yes, he always worked alone."

"Were you home when it happened?" Henry asked, lowering his voice slightly.

"I was shopping at Macy's, when Winston called the store and told me what had happened."

"Winston?" Henry asked.

"He manages the house; you met him earlier," she said, giving a heavy sigh, as she remembered getting the call.

"Winston found the body, I mean, er, your father?" Henry asked, stumbling a bit with his words. That was the question he wanted to ask, but had hoped to be able to do it more delicately.

"We never found a body. Everything was destroyed in the explosion. He was the first one down here, if that is what you mean."

"And you don't have any idea what he was working on?" Henry asked, though he knew the answer.

"No idea at all."

Henry had his answer. A theory was beginning to form, but he was a long way from figuring out where to find the next clue. He needed to get the journal to the district attorney and to find the key that would unravel its contents. He was sure there was something in this house that would point him in the right direction. In his mind there was only one question, *would be able to spot it*? He decided to head back to Mr. Culberson's office and take a closer look at the books. Every clue had been subtle, it seemed reasonable that trend would continue. He would need to talk to Winston.

TWENTY TWO

The Next Clue

Henry walked briskly back through the house, towards the office. Sylvia had difficulty keeping up. The moment he crossed into the office, he stopped and scanned everything, hoping to let the room tell him where to go next. The room wasn't at all talkative. He turned to his left, and started to carefully read the titles, one by one. Mr. Culberson's methodology was to group his books by subject and then, within each subject, they were alphabetical. It was very much a library.

There was a massive section on chess and next to it was a section on puzzles. Henry stopped, sure that the puzzle he was unraveling, must have a clue within these volumes. He pulled each book off the shelf, flipped through it, and looked for anything out of the ordinary. Sylvia watched him for a while, until her curiosity finally got the best of her and she asked, "What are you looking for?"

Henry had forgotten that he wasn't alone, and realized she might be able to help. "I am not sure, but I think there may be a clue here that will help..." He paused before he finished, as he hadn't been entirely truthful with Miss Culberson. She had hired him and paid him well to find the journal, which he had done, and now he needed to make a decision. He continued, "Sylvia, can I trust you?"

She thought the question was rather strange. "Yes, why would you think you couldn't?" She backed up, sensing there was something going on, something she might not like. "Have you found the journal?!" Sylvia demanded.

Henry sensed that he was walking a fine line. He knew that he needed Sylvia, he couldn't let her fly off into a rage, and he must choose his words carefully. He started with, "I have learned something about your father. Please sit down."

"Have you found the Journal? I have paid you well. I demand to know what you are up to! Can you trust me?! The nerve, can I trust you?" She was now in a rage.

It became apparent that he had done a poor job of choosing his first words. Henry was nothing, if not quick on his feet. He took two steps towards her and tightened up his face, "Listen here sweetheart, I found your story to be thin, very thin, I have seen dames like you, and you are all alike. You can either park your cute little butt in that chair and listen to what I have to say or you can go to hell, and try to find your father, on your own!"

This change in approach hit the mark. She was stunned by the last bit and stammered, "Did you say find my father?" She seemed unsteady and Henry helped her to the couch. She was calmer now, so Henry lowered his voice.

"Yes. I don't believe he was killed in the lab. I don't have any proof, and I probably shouldn't have gotten your hopes up, but I needed you to listen," he said and then paused. She didn't say anything, so he continued, "First of all, I don't believe that Mr. Alexander was keeping the journal about your father's business, but they were working together to code the journal, to keep it a secret."

This was very confusing and didn't make any sense to Sylvia, so she asked, "They were working together, but why would an accountant need my father's help?"

"The next part may be hard to understand, perhaps impossible, but I believe that Mr. Alexander had discovered some information, some proof if you will, that would bring down one of the city's most dangerous criminals. I think that your father and Mr. Alexander were planning to turn the journal over to the DA, when someone found out what they were doing. They are both smart men and realized the danger. I believe they may have staged the explosion. It was then…" Henry stopped when he heard the footsteps down the hall.

Sylvia was stunned, but immediately filled with hope. She didn't understand why he had stopped talking, as she hadn't heard the footsteps. "Yes, go on, it was the, what?"

"Winston is coming." Henry said.

"Oh you can trust Winston; he has been with the family since we moved here." She stood up, and ran out to Winston, "Henry thinks that father may still be alive!" she said with glee.

Winston remained unfazed and looked at Henry and said, "You are as clever as Mr. Culberson had hoped."

Sylvia looked shocked, "You knew! Winston!" She was angry, but also thrilled, "It is true then?" She was almost shouting.

"Madame, you must lower your voice. I will try to explain."

Henry let Winston explain, as he went back to the stacks. He went through each of the puzzle books and then it occurred to him that perhaps Winston knew where the next clue was. "Winston, do you have a message for me?"

"Yes sir. Mr. Culberson told me to let you know that he was very interested in animals of late."

"That is the message?" Henry said, hoping for more, but not surprised by its cryptic nature. Undaunted he continued through the stacks until he found a section on the animal kingdom. There were dozens of books. A few books in, Henry noticed that these weren't in alphabetical order by author, but were ordered by species, starting with 'Aardvark Studies', and ending with a thick book about zebras. It seemed that the section contained all the books that had anything to do with animals, fiction and non-fiction combined. Next to the book on beavers, was a book on cows then a book about crows.

Henry paused, *could that be the clue*, as a group of crows are called a murder. He opened it and flipped through the pages. If the clue was there, he didn't get it. Henry continue looking. The Tage Frid clue was one that only he would understand, so he expected the next clue would be similar, and suddenly there it was, a book entitled, 'Fox Habits', sitting to the right of a book 'A Gaggle of Geese'. It was out of order, just by one book, but that, combined with the last present from the closet, meant this had to be the book.

Henry opened to the title page and read the inscription.

Twenty Three

The New Office

Henry pulled out of the drive, the book resting on the passenger seat, and the Four Knights', 'I Get So Lonely', playing on the radio. The steering wheel was cold, really cold, and Henry didn't even notice. His gloves were in his pocket, all warm and napping, just waiting to get in the game. In his mind, he was laying out the cards that had been dealt, looking them over and searching for patterns. It was obvious, at this point, his hand was weak.

Henry reached down and changed the radio station, Frankie Laine & Jimmy Boyd's, 'Tell Me A Story', seemed appropriate, so he stopped searching. Snow began to fall again. The wiper blades seemed to be keeping time. It is one thing to know that one is on the right path; it is an entirely different thing to know where that path is heading. Henry stood on the metaphorical path. It was a maze and though he knew that the 'Goal' was to end up in the DA's office with the journal and the key in hand, he wasn't sure where to turn next. Henry was sure of one thing, if he wasn't careful, and he should get lost in the maze, it could be deadly.

The cityscape changed, he crossed the bridge, the buildings grew and the traffic thickened. Whether it was paranoia, or his aching ribs, Henry kept checking his mirrors. He had a feeling that he was being watched from the moment he left the bridge and arrived in the city. Left, right, left, right,

right and left, put him back on course, and he didn't see anyone, but the feeling persisted.

Henry pulled up to the address on the back of Bobby's card. Henry couldn't believe it. He stood looking up at the Flatiron Building at twenty-third street, famous for its triangular shape and for being responsible for the saying, 'twenty-three skidoo'. The draft from the height and shape of the building had, after the completion in 1902, caused women's skirts to fly up, which meant the local constables had to "skidoo" the men who hung out for a peek. Henry had always hated right angles. He loved a room with character and he had been curious to see the inside of this famous address. For a moment, Henry forgot about his sore ribs, the business card from the future, and the general feeling of being watched.

He walked into the building, climbed the stairs to the third floor and started down the hall. The numbers got larger as he walked; there it was, at the end of the hall, the office which would have the window looking out from the point of the triangle. He hadn't called ahead, as he wanted to check the place out, without Bobby yammering on. Henry reached down and found the door unlocked. He opened it slowly and walked in.

"Hey, Mr. Wood, I am so glad you decided to check the place out. It really suits you. Don't you love the building? You know, the phrase, '23 skidoo' is because of the Flatiron building?"

"Bobby," Henry said, momentarily startled, "Yes, I did know that. What are you…"

"I had a feeling you would be coming over today. I mean, you can't work for too long without an office, can you? You need to find a place fast, and this place is perfect for you.

Here, look around. There is plenty of space out here in the waiting room, for a secretary and a desk, and the office is fantastic, here take a look. I know you will love it." Bobby opened the door, and held it. Henry walked through and it was, indeed, perfect for him. He wasn't about to let Bobby know.

Bobby, a seasoned realtor, was better at reading poker faces than Henry was at wearing one. "I knew it! You do love it. It's perfect for you. You don't have a secretary do you? I know a woman who would be fantastic, she is blonde, types 85 words a minute, and has legs that go on for miles. I can get you her number if you like. Should I get the rental contract?" he asked, and presumably took a breath. Henry thought it was possible that Bobby could talk for hours without stopping or breathing. Henry didn't answer.

He walked around the room, stopping at the window to look down on the street. The room felt like a fortress, which was comforting. He turned around and looked at Bobby, who stood silently; a feat that Henry would have guessed was beyond his abilities. Short, Henry guessed about 5' zero, stout, wearing an old overcoat and a somewhat worn hat, he had a notebook in one pocket, and a racing form was peeking out of the other. His round face seemed honest, even kind, but his constant chatter, made him annoying. Henry stared at Bobby, sizing him up, looking for a clue. Who was this guy? Where did he come from? Why did Sylvia have one of Henry's cards with this address on it? Why was he wearing a coat indoors?

The room was silent, the flow of chatter out of Bobby had completely ceased. After 30 seconds, it was becoming uncomfortable for Henry, he expected that Bobby would start blathering on at any moment, but he didn't. He was mute. Finally Henry decided he wanted to try something and said, "It is ok, but I was wondering if you have anything else in the building, maybe on a different floor?"

"Nope, the building is full; this is the only office available. Shall I get the paperwork?" he responded. He was concise and to the point. This also surprised Henry. He couldn't get a read on Bobby.

Henry said, "I think I would like to think about it for a while?"

Bobby, who was now a paragon of brevity, said "Why?"

Henry knew that he was outmatched. He turned back and looked out the window, as he didn't want the little man to see his smile. He liked Bobby. Henry thought it best to keep that from the strange little man. He also liked the office and since taking the place seemed to be in the cards, he decided not to fight it. "I'll take it."

Bobby made a strange noise, which might have been laughter, Henry wasn't sure. "Great, I have the contract in my office. I knew you would love the place, it is a great building. Oh, you know what? I almost forgot to tell you the best part, aside from being next to the greatest deli in the world, the best part is that my office is right down the hall! We will be neighbors. I know you will love it here. The other tenants are great, except for old man Conner, but don't you worry about him, he keeps to himself. I will get the paper work. I will be right back." He scurried out of the room and silence seemed to hesitantly creep back in, not sure if it was ok.

Henry didn't know how Sylvia had gotten his business cards, which he had yet to print. He didn't know why it was so important he have this office. All he knew is that, like it or not, he had a new friend. From down the hallway, the sound of papers being shuffled, a door creaking as it closed, and someone's radio playing Tony Bennett's hit, "From Rags to Riches", seemed to say that Henry was still on the right path.

TWENTY FOUR

A Brave Face

The traffic was bad enough that he was stopped on the Brooklyn Bridge. He had the window down, despite it being winter and 15 degrees out. He was burning; burning with rage, mad at himself, disgusted that he hadn't considered the ramification of disappearing. Since the office was burned up and his ribs were bruised by Tommy's boys, he had been available to no one. Luna was safely tucked away in his secret house and he had made sure not to contact any of his pals, except Mike.

He thought about Mike, though he didn't want to. He wanted to think about something else. *The sky looks inky blue*, Henry thought to himself. *No, no it isn't; it isn't inky blue at all. It is a bruised and battered blue and purple and black.* Everything he looked at reminded him of Mike. Henry had been calling into the precinct daily and updating Mike about the case. They had decided not to get the journal until the mystery about the code had been worked out.

The newspapers were writing and speculating about where Mr. Alexander was, how he was connected to Tommy 'The Knife', and if Tommy was losing a grip on his organization. A rival family was smelling blood and almost spilled a bit of Tommy's. An attempt had been made, but he had escaped unharmed, though 5 of his boys had not been so lucky. Tommy had immediately retaliated and a pizza parlor, 12 patrons, three of whom were rival thugs, had paid the price. The mayor wanted answers, the police chief worried there was more to come, and the criminal element in the Big Apple was working overtime to find Henry, Mr. Alexander, and the now infamous journal.

Henry knew that hiding Luna was a good idea. He thought that hiding himself seemed reasonable too. What he hadn't counted on was the brutal message that Tommy would deliver through Mike. Sometime late last night, a handful of guys grabbed Mike as he was getting home from working the night shift. They beat him with bats and left him on the front step of his place. Two hours later, he was barely alive. He couldn't even make it up the stairs. This giant of a man just lay there bleeding and broken.

Sally Mae is 11 years old. She is small for her age. She lives next door to 'Big' Mike and adopted him the day he stopped the neighborhood kids from teasing her. From that moment on, if Mike was out on a Saturday, walking to the market, or talking with the neighbors, Sally Mae would be close by, asking him questions and generally worshiping him. Sally Mae didn't know her father; like so many fathers, he had perished on Omaha beach.

When Sally Mae saw Mike, she let out a cry that stopped the neighborhood. Though the ambulance drivers wouldn't let her ride to the hospital with him, nobody had the heart to say she couldn't go with the police officers who were following behind. She sat in the back of the car and sobbed the entire way. It was the most heart-breaking thing either of the officers had ever heard. They could tell she was trying not to, but just couldn't stop herself. When they arrived at the hospital, she sat in the waiting room, head down, weeping into her hands. She didn't stop until they wheeled

Mike out of surgery and into his room. Her mother, the nurses, and even the police chief had all tried to make her feel better, but she just sobbed.

Henry had arrived just as Mike was being wheeled into the room, guarded by two officers. He saw Sally Mae run to the door, stop, take a deep breath, wipe the tears out of her eyes and put a smile on her face. She was being brave for Mike. Neither officer made a move to stop her; they just watched as she went in and gently placed her hand on Mike's. In a tiny voice, without so much as a tremble, she said, "I will take care of you. It is going to be all right." Mike did not hear her, he wasn't conscious yet. Henry thought it was a small blessing, as he was sure that Mike would have felt more pain at seeing Sally's little face, than he ever felt from the beating.

The traffic picked up slightly and Henry eased the car forward. He thought about Mike, though he didn't want to. He thought about little Sally Mae, and her brave face. He thought about the words that Mike had struggled so mightily to get out, after regaining consciousness. "You were right. Important...don't stop now." Henry assumed he was referring to there being someone in the department who was on the take. He didn't know who, and Mike had succumbed to the pain killers before Henry could ask. He didn't think that Mike was in any further danger, as Tommy had been trying to send a message, which he had done.

Night was in full swing, the traffic was moving along nicely, and the lights of the city cast a dim orange glow across the sky. Henry was relieved to find Luna was safe and sound. He filled her in on the day and they sat and talked, and didn't talk, and then mostly they just sat. Just before bed Henry went downstairs and checked the closet. It was filled with goodies. He laid them out on his bench and looked at them. It must be a clue. He was too tired to figure it out though, so he flipped off the light switch and went upstairs to bed.

TWENTY FIVE

Captain Donnelley

Captain Donnelley had worked his way up from beat cop, been a detective for 12 years, and then promoted to captain. When word came down about Mike, he cancelled all time off and mobilized every man in the precinct. It wasn't just an attack on one of their own, it was on one of their best and most loved. The squad room was packed and buzzed with the din of anger and speculation. Donnelley wasn't much on making speeches, but he liced listening to a good one. In the captain's mind, a gooh speaker is a man to be respected. He considered it his great weakness, because the right words can move men to push themselves beyond their best, to something unstoppable. This was a time when he needed to get it right.

"Everyone listen up." The room quieted. "As you all know by now Mike is in the hospital. He's in bad shape, but I am told he should make it." A restrained cheer went up, but the captain waved his hand for silence. He had much more to say and everyone settled down. "This wasn't just an attack on Mike, it was an attack on the badge."

There were nods of agreement.

"I want Mike's neighborhood canvassed, then I want every scumbag in the city rousted. Get me answers and get them now."

To a man there was a sense of urgency. The speech, while not especially eloquent, hit the mark. Some of the men had just finished their shifts, but were staying; two of them were coming off a double and were staying too. There weren't any complaints and each was ready to scour the city to find those responsible.

"One more thing, don't take anything for granted. Right now all we know is Mike was beaten by, at the very least, three guys. This might be the start of something bigger. Watch each other's backs." The captain paused and took a breath,"l want every man is to keep their gun with them at all times. The sergeant will take it from here."

The noise started up again. The sergeant had a map of Mike's neighborhood up on the wall. Other boards, containing photos of all the people killed in the gang wars, were pushed aside. Some thought that it was related, but they agreed that it was best to consider every angle.

TWENTY SIX

Tommy Gets His Nickname

Tommy kissed his wife goodnight, mostly out of habit. He didn't like her much anymore, nor did she care for him. She found him revolting, but they were devout Catholics and had learned to tolerate each other over the years. Tommy left. He said he was going for a drive, but she knew he wouldn't be back until morning. It was fine with her.

The snow was pretty bad, but he didn't care, he just needed to think. Since the day he gutted his first scumbag for finking to the cops, he had wanted to be the boss. Now it seemed like it wasn't so much fun anymore.

Killing came easy to Tommy. He viewed it as a gift. He remembered watching other guys get their first kill. They would be shaken up, trying to hide it and look tough, but wanting to get sick. He always knew that when it was his turn, he would be much stronger.

Tommy drove along through the snow and remembered those early days. At 19, there were but a few brokern arms on the resume. He was eager to get his chance and would often daydream about what it was going to be like. He pictured the look on the guy's face. He could hear him begging for his life. Tommy would let him go on for a bit and maybe let the poor bastard think he had a chance, then 'bang' right in the forehead. Other guys would make them turn around first, shoot them in the back of the head, but not Tommy, he wanted to look the guy in the eyes.

His first kill hadn't gone at all like he had imagined.

Jimmy, his first boss and as it would later turn out, his 22nd kill, called him into the office. "I need you to go take care of that Polack on 82nd Street; the one with the dry cleaners. He has some unfortunate debts and we gonna make an example of him. You know the guy?"

Tommy knew who it was and couldn't wait. Three other guys, much older, went along, but it was Tommy who was to pull the trigger. It was a test. The guys gave him a hard time about 'bustin his cherry'. Tommy just sat in the back and took it, because that was part of the deal. They laughed, betting on whether his hand would shake, before pulling the trigger and one guy joked he might wet himself.

When they mentioned the gun, Tommy felt sick. His gun wasn't loaded. He had been cleaning it when Jimmy called and left the bullets at home. The rest of the drive he tried to figure out what to do. He couldn't ask for bullets, the ridicule would be unbearable. If he did, he was sure they would start calling him 'Tommy Blanks' or something like that. It was the sort of nickname which he would never be able to wipe off.

He was still thinking about it when they arrived at the apartment. The four of them walked in and the man turned white. The three older guys started talking about how he owed them money and his time was up. He pleaded for his life. They laughed. After a while the moment had arrived and Tommy didn't hesitate. He took a heavy kitchen knife and standing behind the guy, reached around and plunged it into is gut. The man gasped and Tommy wrapped him in a bear hug. When the final shudder passed, he lifted him up on his shoulder and said, "Let's go"

The three old guys were stunned. They just stood there looking at this kid, his pants covered in blood, as his shoulder turned crimson. Then one of them said, "Tommy 'The Knife' just popped his cherry"

The other two roared and patted him on the back. The name had stuck.

Tommy walked up to his girlfriend's apartment and pounded three times. She was on the couch sleeping, the radio was on, and she said sleepily, "Coming." She opened the door, wearing a silk robe, loosely tied. He wandered in, feeling anxious, and went straight for the bar. She followed him and wrapped her arms around his chest, "You came over to visit me. I love a surprise visit."

"You're my girl." He dropped a couple of ice cubes into the glass and poured the scotch, his mind still thinking about the journal. "What you been up to doll?"

"I was listening to the radio, but fell asleep. You want to take me dancing?"

"Nah, we staying in tonight. I got some thinking to do."

She knew better than to ask about his business, so she went into the kitchen to make him something to eat.

Tommy knew what his next move was; he didn't need to discuss it with Sal. He would send some of his boys out in the morning. Once it was set right in his head, he relaxed. His girl brought him a sandwich and they sat on the couch for a while, and then went to bed.

TWENTY SEVEN

Eddie's Garage

It started as an attack at the restaurant, which led to Tommy's rebuttal. Once the blood started to spill, it became a flood. Within a few days it had escalated to the point where two families were now vying for Tommy's head, and his turf. The Isle of Manhattan was on edge. The papers were covered with reports of the violence, some of it not actually related to the fighting. Everybody feared it would only get worse.

Tommy had lost 13 men; there were another 20 or so wounded. He had the largest crew, but fighting two families was taking its toll. Morale was low. Most of his men were running on adrenaline, afraid of the next attack, and even more terrified of Tommy's rage.

On Long Island, with six bays, Eddie's Garage is where they all go. He fixes the cars, repairs the holes and has had a poker game running for longer than anyone can remember. Eddie Jr. runs the garage now, as his father passed away in '47. Eddie senior was a loud and well liked man. Eddie junior is more reserved, but he and his crew get the job done.

Bones got his nickname from rolling 'the bones'. He never met a game of craps he didn't like. Today they played poker. Bulldog, Joe and Nicky Toes, sat in the corner of the garage, smoking cigars. An old pool table lamp hung over the table at an odd angle. Behind them there was a Coke machine and a wash basin filled with ice and beers. The sound of tools was mixed with the laughter and swearing of the game.

The doors to bays four and five opened up and two black sedans, which had seen better days, rolled in. Sal and his driver got out of one and two men got out of the other. The mechanics all stopped working when Nicky Toes racked a shotgun. Joe, Bulldog and Bones drew their guns. Bones knocked his chair to the floor, when he jumped up, making a horrible racket. Sal's three guys all had their guns out too. There was a great silence in the garage. Eddie almost said something, but Sal walked forward, "I'm off the clock. We can shoot each other tomorrow."

Bones gave a nod and his guys put their guns down. "Beer?"

Sal didn't say anything, which was his norm, but he did smile and took one from the tub. He popped off the cap and took out a wad of bills, "Deal me in."

The tension was gone and the noise of bullet holes being fixed and engines under repair, returned to their normal levels.

Twenty Eight

The District Attorney's Office

Henry walked into the D.A's office. The secretary asked for his name and quickly popped her head into the boss's office. She told Henry he could go right in. District Attorney Mark McKinley had been in his job for longer than most. He didn't seem to have the political aspirations that many of his predecessors possessed. Standing and shaking Henry's hand, he smiled broadly. They had met before but this was the first time Henry had been in his office. Mark offered Henry a seat and sat back down behind his desk.

Mark McKinley was popular around town. He could trace his lineage directly to the 25th President of the United States, William McKinley. Mark had graduated at the top of his class from Michigan Law and been a young star in NY from the day he wandered into his first courtroom. Combining handsome and charming, with brains, had made him unstoppable. Few were surprised when he became the youngest D.A. the city had seen, and he settled into a comfortable life.

"It is good to see you, Henry. Frankly, I have been expecting you. Mike said you had some proof, a journal or something, which is going to put Tommy 'The Knife' behind bars for a good long time."

"I don't have it with me. But I can get it," Henry said.

"Why didn't you bring it with you? I need that journal, I can't convene a grand jury without it, and things are getting pretty bad around here," Mark said, in a voice that struck Henry as less than calm.

"I am playing this one close to the vest. There is too much at stake. When I am ready, I will bring the journal to you."

"Listen here Henry, if you are withholding evidence, I will throw you in the can and you can rot there," Mark said, standing and pounding his fist on his desk.

Henry didn't move, nor was he moved by the threat. "Who knows about the journal, other than the three of us?"

"I haven't told anyone. I only found out a couple of days ago myself. Now are you going to give it over or what?" Mark said. An awkward silence hung in the room. He sat back down, realizing that Henry wasn't going to be intimidated.

"You know what happened to Mike, I assume," Henry said, leaning forward and lowering his voice.

"Of course," Mark whispered back.

"I am not anxious to get found by Tommy and I don't know who to trust. Are you sure you can keep the journal safe?"

"I guarantee it. Now when do I get it?" Mark said, in a hurried voice.

"I have a couple of things to work out..." Henry paused, and then continued," I don't think it is safe for me to be wandering around your office, can you meet me tomorrow night?"

"Yes, sure, where and when?" Mark said, seeming suddenly at ease.

Henry grabbed the yellow pad and wrote down the address of his new office and 11 PM on the pad and slid it back across the desk, then said, "Come alone, as I said, I don't trust anyone."

Henry got up and left without another word. The secretary was filing her nails as he walked out and didn't bother to look up. Forty minutes later Henry sat down across from Luna and a piping hot pizza.

"What did he say?" Luna asked

"About what I would expect. He wants the journal," Henry said, grabbing a slice of pie. "Did you get a hold of Sylvia and Winston?"

"Yes. They are being careful and they will meet us at your office," Luna said with a slight tone to her voice.

"Is there something wrong?"

"No."

Henry let it go, and they ate in silence. There were still a lot of things to do and not much time, and he knew the odds were stacked against them. Henry had made a list when he got up in the morning. Visit the D.A. was at the top. There were still quite a few more items that needed to be crossed off, and they would need to get started after the pizza was gone.

TWENTY NINE

Francis Visits The Hospital

Francis Le Mange had known Mike since he met Henry. Though the three of them would occasionally have a few beers together, he and Mike always seemed to be at odds. As a rule, the mere sight of Mike put him in a mood to argue.

Francis sat in the waiting room with a dozen or so of Mike's friends. He didn't know any of them. There was a small elderly catholic woman, who after praying with her rosary, had picked up a Sports Illustrated. Two couples huddled around a small table and spoke in hushed tones. The rest seemed to be alternating between sitting and standing, hoping a change would stifle some of the worry.

The rallying of support cast a new light on the man. Francis doubted that, if it were he, there would have been more than a few visitors. Then he felt guilty for thinking about himself. Now it was his turn. The two officers watching the door were reporting directly to Sally Mae. She allowed each visitor no more than five minutes. As soon as she sensed Mike getting tired, the visits ended.

Francis set the flowers among the others. "You are looking a little rough."

Sally Mae gave Francis an angry look and crossed her arms. Mike smiled, "I've been better, but Sally Mae is taking good care of me. I'll be back in the game before you know it."

"I am sure you will. You are a tough cookie."

"Leave it to you to speak in food."

Francis smiled, "It is what I do." Then there was silence.

Neither of the men was sure how to have a civil conversation with the other. Sally Mae sensed that it was getting uncomfortable, so she announced that it was time for Mike to rest.

Francis went home and rolled a sheet of paper into his Underwood. It had been his dream to write a novel someday, but fear and self loathing had kept the dream at bay. With his head in turmoil, he turned to his words and began. It didn't go well. Without any real ideas for a plot or characters, he wondered aimlessly across the page. Before long he had a poor man's Faulkner running for a couple of pages. He read it and thought to himself, *stream of unconsciousness*, rip and crumple.

Nothing came of his writing session, save for a much deeper desire to write beyond the inches allowed by his editor. He dressed and went out for dinner, but the sadness for Mike persisted. He would go see him again tomorrow.

THIRTY

The Long Wait

Luna had asked Sylvia and Winston to come to Henry's office around 2:00 pm. She hadn't told them why, mostly because she didn't know. Henry had a plan, and she trusted him. After they had finished lunch, she and Henry had gone back to his sparsely furnished office and he had asked her to keep an eye on things while he took a walk to clear his head. She thought to herself that it was a pretty easy task, as there wasn't much to look at, save for the painting of the White House that hung on the wall in the outer room. Henry had once mentioned that he liked fine art, and this was not an example of such but did give the artist credit for having captured the essence of 'better than a blank wall'. So she sat and kept an eye on this wholly unremarkable painting.

Henry had a plan. Actually he had a vague idea of something that might work or may completely blow up in his face. After the beating Mike had taken, he didn't feel that he could continue to search for the missing pieces of the codex. He needed to make a move. Tommy 'The Knife' appeared to be getting desperate, the rival gangs seemed to think that this was the time for an all out war to topple Tommy. The constant speculation in the newspapers was turning the city of Manhattan into a powder keg that was about to blow.

Henry walked a little bit further and came to the familiar steps of the Library, which held the key to it all. It was unseasonably warm today and the snow that had covered everything was now a gray melting coat of sludge. He stopped and lit a cigarette, casually puffing on it, while he looked around to see if anyone might have followed him. Henry didn't smoke, but he always kept a pack of Lucky Strikes on him, and a lighter, for just such an occasion. The little white sticks gave one a perfect excuse for stopping anywhere and pausing to take a drag or two.

It was clear that nobody cared about Henry, so he flicked the butt into the gutter and went into the library. He stopped at the card catalog and waited a few more minutes. If anyone were following him, they would move quickly to get inside, lest they lose him. Nobody else passed through the doors so he felt safe. Back into the stacks he went, past rows and rows of books about everything known to man. He loved the smell of books and the sounds of a library. Everyone thinks of libraries as being perfectly quiet, but they aren't, they have their own language. The chatter of chair legs on marble floors, pages being turned, muffled whispers at tables with overworked students, and the echo of feet walking here and there, were like a quiet sonata to his ears. Henry normally found it comforting. Today, he listened for anything out of the ordinary and took no comfort in bringing the journal from its hiding place.

Down the steps, past more rows, right turn, left turn, past some study tables, and down another hall. Two more flights of stairs down, and finally he arrived in a section barely visited, filled with rare books on economic theory, mathematics, and science. He pulled out the 'Principles of Political Economy and Taxation', a first edition from 1817, by David Ricardo. It had slightly less dust than its brethren on either side, and behind this rare and wonderful tome, which explains labor theory of value, rested the journal. Henry pulled the journal out, wrapped a small towel around it, which he had brought with him, and tucked it under his overcoat. He indulged himself with a brief glance at Ricardo's masterpiece, and then he lightly blew the dust off and carefully placed it back on the shelf.

He walked back through the library and exited into the afternoon damp. A light rain waited. The sky was darkening, and there was a general air of dread all about. Maybe it was just his own dread he was sensing? Henry was especially alert now. He had the journal and worried that he might get jumped by some of Tommy's thugs before he could meet with the DA. He covered the distance between the library and his office in half the normal time. Up two flights of stairs and down the hall, almost running, Henry was glad to be back to the office.

When he opened the door he saw that Winston and Sylvia had arrived. Winston was examining the painting, while Sylvia and Luna were sitting at the receptionist desk chatting. They turned to Henry with a collective, 'Did you get the book?' look on their faces. Henry gave a nod and walked into his office. Gathering around the desk, they shared a sense of anticipation and dread. He brought forth the journal as if it were as fragile as bone china. Carefully Henry took off the wrapping and set it down for them all to see.

There was silence for a few minutes as the four of them looked at it and marveled at all the trouble such a little notebook had caused. When Henry finally spoke, all he said was, "Ok, I hope this works." They all nodded solemnly and got settled in for a long afternoon.

THIRTY ONE

The Weight Of Time

The afternoon had slipped away. Henry felt the weight of time, as if each grain through the hourglass had been piling upon his shoulder. The wait was almost unbearable. He wondered if D.A., Mark McKinley, would be on time. He suspected he might be early, but with it already being 10:45 pm, that ship was almost out of the harbor. So he sat, feet up on the desk. His left hand mindlessly tapped a, well chewed, Dixon Ticonderoga against the edge of the open drawer.

The drawer was the second one down on the left side of the desk. It wasn't open very far; just far enough that he could see his revolver laying there, waiting to be called upon if needed. The gun didn't seem at all concerned with the passage of time, or the stakes of the gamble he was taking. It has just one job, it knows its job, and it will do it when called upon, end of story.

Slowly, tap, tap, tap. Henry listened to the sound of traffic outside. The window was shut, but a city like New York doesn't let itself be muffled by a lousy window. The familiar wail of 'Taxi', the splashing of puddles, the honking of horns, all shouted that the Big Apple was alive and well, going about its business. The city was marching to its own beat of time, as it had for longer than Henry had been there, and he knew it would be there long after he had gone.

10:46 and Henry thought about the closet. He wondered where it went to, its relationship to time. The last clues, which he hadn't had time to truly study, puzzled him. He thought about why he hadn't had time to study the bevy of tools, and how Mike was still lying in a hospital, broken. He thought about the little girl willing him back to health.

The pencil paused; did he hear someone coming down the hall? He listened, then the muted banging of a door, somewhere near the other end, closing, and the faint metal clicking of the lock being turned. Then the footsteps walking away and only the city noises remained. Tap, Tap, Tap started the pencil again, finding the same measure of time, and settling back into waiting.

Winston stood in a doorway, down from the office, his collar turned up against the cold night air. He could see the little restaurant down the street where Sylvia sat at the window. She was not eating, more nibbling on her food, her senses were alive and she made sure that she saw everything passing outside. As the hour approached 11:00 she felt her stomach tightening. Luna had gotten a room at a hotel the other direction from Henry's office and had perched in the window. She could see the entire street and the alley behind the strange triangular building. They had all the angles covered.

When the pencil stopped this time, Henry set it down. The soft leather of expensive shoes was padding its way down the hall. He was early, but not so much as to seem desperate. Henry didn't like the DA. He didn't like the way he wielded his power, and he didn't like the way he hadn't even asked how Mike was doing.

There was a pause just outside the door. A slight shuffling as if the DA was checking to see if he was at the right office, and then he turned the knob and walked in, like a cat who was up to no good. Henry had left the door between his office and the outer office open. When the DA walked in, Henry stood slowly and walked over to shake his hand. He grabbed the outstretched hand warmly with both hands, displaying not a sign of his dislike.

"I see you made it," Henry said, and returned back behind the desk.

"Yes, you thought I wouldn't?" the DA asked, removing his hat.

"No, I knew you would show up. This is too important. Did anyone follow you?"

"Follow me? No, why? Nobody knows I am coming here, why would they?" he replied with more verve than seemed appropriate, and the DA sensed he was going on a bit, and quickly regained his composure and demanded, "So let's have it." His voice was now much more measured.

This only seemed to confirm Henry's suspicion. The effort the DA was making to control his emotions and to hide the secret agenda, Henry suspected, made it clear. Henry pulled the drawer further open, reached past the revolver, and removed the journal. He looked at it for a moment, just to see if Mr. McKinley might get anxious again. He didn't and Henry handed it across the desk.

"You have done a great thing Mr. Wood; this will be the end of Tommy and his gang. Now I've got them," he said as he opened the journal and held it under the desk lamp. He flipped a few pages and then a few more. "This looks like it is some sort of code."

"It is. That is what has been taking me so long. I have been looking for the codex which will let me break it." Henry said, sitting down and leaning back in his chair.

"You don't have the key?" the DA exclaimed, not seeming too concerned.

"No, and I don't know where it is. But I will keep looking."

"Good, good, of course we can't proceed until we know what this says, but at least it is safe now," he calmly stated as he closed the journal up and tucked it into his coat. "Thanks again, Mr. Wood, for keeping this safe; the city appreciates it."

"Yes, well, I will keep looking for the key, and when I find it, you can lock that bastard, Tommy, up." Henry stood and the DA quickly shook his hand and said softly, "You don't worry about a thing, Mr. Wood; I will take care of it."

And, with that, he left. Henry listened to the footsteps walking down the hall and stood by the window to watch which way he left the building. A moment later, the DA exited onto the street below, looked around nervously and then turned to the left. He was heading towards Luna's vantage point. Henry hoped he was wrong about the DA, but he knew, in his gut, he wasn't.

THIRTY TWO

Corruption

There wasn't much to look at now. The DA was out of sight almost immediately, but Henry still stood and looked down to the street, almost in a trance. He was sure the next few minutes would be important; he hoped he had misjudged the DA, because that would make life a good deal easier. Henry was shaken out of his daze by the ringing.

He grabbed the phone and put it to his ear.

"I see him, Henry; he is going into the alley," Luna said.

"Can you see all the way to the other end of the street?" Henry asked.

"Almost, but there is a car half way down, and 4 men just got out of it. They look serious."

"Keep watching," Henry instructed, feeling certain he knew what was coming.

Luna continued her commentary, "Ok, the men are standing by the car doors; Mr. McKinley is still walking towards them. The driver has just walked out to meet him. They look like they are talking. He just handed the man the journal and ohhh," Luna gasped.

"What is it?"

"The man he gave the journal to, just hit him. He went down and now the other guys are dragging him to the side of the alley. Oh, one guy just kicked him," Luna exclaimed with concern.

"Don't worry Luna; I am sure he is ok. I suspected this was his game."

"Ok," she said in a quiet voice, obviously upset by the violence.

"You best head back to the office; I'm going to go and get Sylvia and Winston. I'll be back shortly."

Henry hung up the phone after he heard something resembling an ok, but much quieter. His suspicion had been confirmed; the leak in the department was the District Attorney. Henry walked around the desk, reached towards the lamp, but decided to leave it on for Luna. Henry put on his overcoat and hat and walked out of the office. He listened to his own shoes; they didn't sound the same as the DA's expensive ones, and he wondered if he should check on him. Though he now hated the DA, and knew that Mike lay in the hospital because of his betrayal, he wanted to make sure the thugs hadn't been too rough. Henry wanted Mr. McKinley to be alive and well. He needed Mr. McKinley to think that Henry believed he was robbed by some random thugs. Henry thought he should go check on him, but decided he just didn't want to. He was sure that the DA would have planned for this, and that there would be a phone call tomorrow, explaining what had happened and how they were doing everything in their power to recover the journal.

Though Henry didn't like thinking about the DA being corrupt, it did mean one thing. Tommy would back off now. He had the journal and life would return to normal. Actually that wasn't entirely true; Tommy had 'a' journal, not 'the' journal.

Winston, with the help of Luna and Sylvia, meticulously made up a journal filled with jumbled letters and numbers, and now Tommy 'The Knife' would get a coded journal, just as he was expecting. Once he burned it, the problem would be almost completely solved, except for the one loose end. The loose end, of course, was Luna's father.

Henry didn't know where Luna and Sylvia's fathers were, but he figured that if Tommy's boys hadn't been able to find them yet, they were probably safe. The plan is simple now. Find the rest of the codex and unravel the real journal. Once Henry knew what Luna's father had on Tommy, he would be able to play the end game. He would be able to get justice for Mike and put Tommy and the DA behind bars for the remainder of their lives.

Henry waved to Winston across the street, and then knocked on the window where Sylvia was on the lookout. As the three of them walked back to the office, Henry brought them up to speed. Neither, Winston nor Sylvia, had much to say. Something about learning that the DA is in cahoots with the worst gangster in town had dampened their mood considerably.

Luna was sitting on the edge of the desk when they got back. Henry laid out his plan for putting things right. He wanted to sound confident that everything would turn out just fine, but he didn't think he could pull it off, so he just said his piece and they called it a day. Tomorrow they would all gather and look over the most recent clue.

Thirty Three

After The Fall

Luna, Winston and Sylvia stood in the hall as Henry locked the door. The idea that the District Attorney was on the take hadn't fully sunk in. His fall from grace was just the start, and they all knew it. Sylvia broke the silence, "I could use a drink," Luna nodded in agreement.

Winston chimed in, "I could go for a spot of brandy, and perhaps a bite to eat. I am feeling a bit peckish."

"Charlie's is just down the block, it is quiet, and I know the owner. He will be happy to fire up the grill," Henry said, as he turned around and led everyone down the hall.

They came out onto the street; an ambulance rushed past them, and headed towards the alley. The lights of half a dozen patrol cars painted the sides of the building with frantic movement. People were starting to gather around to see what had happened. Henry and the others walked in the opposite direction, towards Charlie's, a stiff drink, and the start of the next chapter in their lives.

The preceding days had been especially trying; the fire at his old office, getting jumped by Tommy's thugs, and seeing Big Mike all broken and bruised. It had taken it's toll on Henry. Bad as it had been, it was nothing compared to what Sylvia and Luna had been going through, not knowing what had become of their fathers and living each day in fear. Henry was glad Winston was around. Though he was older, he had assured Henry that he could keep an eye on her, as he had been a crack shot in the war.

The room smelled of cheap cigars and loneliness, and was mostly empty. A pool table in the back had two sticks lying across it and looked like it had seen better days. The bartender, Charlie, was wiping a dirty glass with a dirtier dishtowel. He looked up, shifted the toothpick from one side of his mouth to the other, and nodded at Henry.

"Hey Charlie, can you fire up the grill for my friends? We've had a long day."

"How about some steaks?"

Henry looked at Luna; she said quietly, "Sounds good to me," and she looked at the others. Sylvia and Winston didn't put forth any objection and slid into the booth by the jukebox.

As Winston took a sip of brandy, which Charlie had begrudgingly served him, Harry, Luna and Sylvia drank their ice-cold beers in silence. Luna said it first, but they were all thinking the same thing, "What do we do now?"

Henry took a pull from his beer. He had known that this moment would come. He had to tell them about the closet and what his gut was telling him. "I have something to tell you, and your inclination to think I am crazy, is, well, to be expected."

Sylvia smiled and with her sultry voice, "Oh Henry, we would never think you are crazy." She reached across the table and took his hand. Luna took a pull of her beer and looked off into space. Henry continued, "I had been drinking a lot a few months back. Business had been slow and so I spent my days down in my shop, and my nights, well, mostly here. One night when I went home I had passed out on the couch in the basement, and I thought I was dreaming when I heard the sounds coming from the closet. I woke up and just stared at it. There was a brief flash and then the sound stopped. I was sure I had been dreaming, but I decided to look anyway. All of the old boxes were gone. The interior was spotless and on the shelf sat a magazine."

"A magazine, sir?" Winston said, raising one eyebrow as he swirled the brandy in its snifter.

"Yes, it was a copy of Sport magazine..." Henry paused and took a sip from his beer, "...the November...1955 issue to be exact." He paused to let this sink in.

Winston seemed to be a bit skeptical of his claim, "November of this year, eleven months from now?" He took a sip of his brandy. Sylvia and Luna looked at each other and then back to Henry. Charlie brought over their dinners and set them on the table. Nobody started eating, and Henry continued, "I didn't believe it myself. It said the Brooklyn Dodgers win the World Series and Johnny Podres will win something called the MVP."

Sylvia smiled, "The Dodgers beat the Yankees? Now I know you are kidding."

Henry reached up and pulled the magazine from the inside pocket of his overcoat, which was draped over the back the booth. He dropped it on the table. Nobody touched the magazine; they just looked at the cover and the date. Henry took a few bites of his steak. Slowly each of them started to eat, and Charlie hollered from behind the bar, "How's the grub?" Everyone raised their drinks in a toast to the chef. Charlie went back to fiddling around with the glasses.

Henry continued, "There's more. The magazine wasn't the only thing that showed up from the future. Over the next few weeks, periodically there would be all sorts of interesting things, mostly tools. It was as if the future knew what I needed. After a while, I just accepted that I had a benefactor, but I didn't know who it was or why I had been chosen. That is, until I started receiving clues regarding your fathers' case."

They all listened and ate and theorized about how it might work. Henry felt better having shared his secret. Luna reasoned that it was their fathers who had been sending the clues. Henry wasn't sure, but felt it had given her hope and kept his opinion to himself. The rest of the evening was spent drinking and even laughing. By the time Charlie was ready to close up, they were all pretty liquored up, and so Charlie called a cab for Sylvia and Winston, while Henry and Luna went back to the room in the hotel.

Henry opened the door. Luna walked in and spun around and flung her arms around Henry. "You have been wonderful. I can't thank you enough." Then she gave him a big kiss, and Henry let her. Luna looked into Henry's eyes, then excused herself and went into the bathroom. Henry walked over and looked out the window. The police were still milling about. There were a few photographers trying to talk their way into the alley. The police kept everyone at bay. Henry heard Luna come out of the bathroom, but didn't turn around. Playing the whole evening over again, in his head, he wondered how much the thugs had roughed up the DA. He was sure that it was likely just a few good pokes, for show, but he hoped it had stung. The papers would be all over this, and if Henry was right, the balance of power would be restored. Tommy's gang, with the journal in hand, wouldn't feel threatened, and thus their strangle hold on the Big Apple crime scene would be secure. This meant the other gangs would stop trying to take over and Tommy wouldn't have any reason to go after Luna or her father.

But it wasn't over, not by a long shot. He turned around and on the bed, splayed out, was a very much passed out Luna. He put a blanket over her and returned to the window. As he watched the city, the sky started to sprinkle a fresh coat of snow over the filth below. He pulled the worn November issue of Sport magazine out of his pocket as he laid his coat over the back of the chair. As Luna slept, he read again how his beloved Dodgers were going to put it to the Yankees.

THIRTY FOUR

Mark McKinley Beaten

Mark McKinley lay in the alley with some cracked ribs and a busted lip. He thought he might have a concussion, so he focused on staying conscious. The ambulance arrived after a few minutes, closely followed by a legion of patrol cars. He felt the January cold grabbing him, he wanted to sleep, but the medics kept bothering him.

On the ride to the hospital he thought about his wife and kids briefly. He imagined them standing by his bed. The still images, in his mind, made him think about the news. He could milk the attack and get some sympathy press. The idea of running for Mayor or Governor had never been one he had entertained. If he were to consider it though, this would be the time. The sirens sure were loud. He wondered if they would make him stay the night. What time was it anyway? He closed his eyes and the man next to him started yelling again. He really wanted to grab a quick nap. What about the Mayor's office? It could be possible. If he was the governor, though, and made deals with the five families, he might have a shot at the Presidency. Nobody would need to know; he could keep crime at an acceptable level, and be a hero. The families would listen, he was sure of it; he had just saved the day.

The doctors determined that it was a very mild concussion and after a dozen stitches and some taped ribs, he was given some pain medication and allowed to sleep. The wife and kids were being brought to the hospital and there were two uniformed officers standing guard outside his room.

"This ain't right."

"I know, I'm coming off a double shift and I get stuck on door duty."

"No, I mean the DA getting mugged."

"Oh that. I suppose. What was he doing wondering around alone like that, doesn't he have a driver?"

"He does. Maybe he gave him the night off. I hear he is a really easy going guy."

"I don't know him."

"I've talked to him a few times. After that big B & E case, we had a cup of coffee. He said I was well on my way to making detective one day."

"It's good to have friends in high places."

"He seems like a regular guy," then whispered, "of course, you can never tell with lawyers."

They both laughed, and then started talking about their families, nurses, and baseball.

THIRTY FIVE

Tommy Gets The Journal

Sal handed the journal to Tommy. He flipped it over, looked at the back and then sat down. Flipping each page carefully, he studied the entries and then leaned back in his chair.

The room was quiet for several minutes. "That's all fellas." He gave a look to Sal who knew to stay behind. The other three filed out and Sal said, "Tell em', I got the first round." The three guys headed down to the bar, while Sal waited for Tommy to share what was on his mind. There was always something, usually it was off the mark, sometimes it was just paranoid and crazy, but he would let him talk and nod. Sal closed the door.

Tommy, "You take a look at this?"

"No."

Tommy stood up and handed it to Sal. He got a drink while Sal sat down and read through the first few pages. Tommy poured himself a bourbon, "You want one?"

"Sure," though he didn't.

Tommy poured another and handed it to Sal, "What do you think?"

Sal didn't know why, but it seemed off somehow. He wasn't ready to tell Tommy, though, "I think the accountant was stupid for crossing you."

"Any problems with the DA tonight?"

"He was a few minutes late, but it was fine, nobody was around. He gave it to me and then we roughed him up, just like you said."

"How'd he take it?"

"Didn't say a word."

"So McKinley can take a punch, eh?" Tommy laughed a little.

"He took em pretty good, but he knew they were coming. I don't think he could throw a punch though, probably be crap at collections."

This made Tommy roar. "I could just see that little mic bastard trying to make the rounds, they'd chew him up and spit him out."

"Why you think the accountant wrote the whole damn thing in code. You think he knew we would eventually find out?"

Sal just shrugged as he handed it back to Tommy. "You want me to put the word out that we got it back?"

"Yeah, let em know. We can get back to business." He started to flip through it again, sipping his bourbon as he turned the pages. "You think this is the original?"

"What do you mean?" Sal asked, because he knew Tommy liked to talk. Sal had been thinking the same thing, it seemed off, but he didn't want to put that idea in Tommy's head. If it got there on its own, fine, but he wasn't going to add to his paranoia.

"It is too clean," Tommy said, and then turned on his desk lamp to look closer. "You think the DA might be holding out on us?"

"How so?" Sal liked to let Tommy fill in the blanks. It avoided confusion.

"Maybe he's thinking he might like to be mayor or renegotiate terms."

"I don't think he has the balls to cross you, boss. You scare the shit out of him."

Tommy smiled, not looking up from the journal.

"But maybe he keeps it for insurance?" Sal suggested.

"You think we should have a little chat with Mr. McKinley?" Tommy asked, but not really.

"Sure, I can go talk to him. He ain't gonna try anything right away, though. If he was, he wouldn't have taken the beating. If you want to know what I think…" Sal paused for Tommy's reaction.

Tommy just looked up, listening. He respected Sal and though he didn't talk much, when he did, it was usually worth hearing him out. Tommy didn't listen to anyone else.

"I say we give it a few days, let the word get out that this mess is behind us, then arrange one of your dinners."

Tommy closed the journal and stood up to lock it in the safe. He wasn't going to destroy it, yet. "I like that. He'll be expecting something anyway. We feed him, give him some booze, and then when his guard is down, start asking questions."

Sal knew the meeting was over and went down to the bar. Giving the order, to a couple of guys, to spread the word, he got a coke from the bartender and read the rest of the day's paper. It was back to business as usual, just the way Sal liked it.

THIRTY SIX

Double Play

Not everyone is able to tell when they are in a dream, some people only part of the time, and for Henry it was almost never. Tonight, he had started out playing for his beloved Dodgers, actually he was on the bench sitting next to Karl Spooner. The Dodgers were up to bat in the bottom of the 5th and Roy Campanella had just hit a one out home run and was returning to the bench. He sat a few feet away, and was putting his gear back on. Henry knew it was a dream, but didn't care. Karl was talking to him, just like he was one of the guys; he was complaining how sore his right arm was, caused by his start the day before. Henry said to Karl, "Yeah my neck is bothering me, must have wrenched it when I slid into second." Karl said that he thought it was great the way Henry had broken up that double play and kept the inning alive. Just then the crack of the bat caused Henry to look out into the field and see...

The window had made a cracking sound as it was being buffeted by the fierce snowstorm outside. Henry glanced at his watch and it was 2:47 am; he had been asleep for only a half hour or so. He shifted around in the chair, pulled his overcoat back over him, and drifted off again. The next few hours were filled with moments, some happy, some terrifying, some just plain bizarre. The last dream was in a huge library. The stacks were, at first, like the ones he had seen when he went to Sylvia's and had found the book in her father's collection. Then he was among the books where he had hidden the journal, and finally he had been standing in a strange place filled with towers of books and magazines. They weren't on shelves, but stacked and piled all about a massive room. Henry could see rows and paths, which had been created among the mountains of books, and he found himself wandering through them with a feeling of helplessness. He saw a book that he suspected might contain a clue, but the hundreds of books on top of it were too heavy for him to pull it out. Each time he tried, the stack would start to sway. He was sure that if it fell on him he would be crushed. He gave it a final pull and...

He woke up feeling like he had been crushed by a stack of books. His head was pounding, and every muscle ached from sleeping in a ball on the chair. He looked over at Luna; she was lying on her side, hugging the pillow, with a little smile running across her face. Her look of calm was unsettling to Henry. She trusted him. Luna truly believed that everything was going to be all right, and she counted on him to make it happen. Henry felt a chill run through his body. Doubt started screaming in his head. Or was that the hangover? He couldn't be sure.

He got up quietly and went into the bathroom. The haggard looking man in the mirror didn't look like he played for Brooklyn. Of all the dreams the night before, that was the one that remained with him, that and something about books. He turned the faucet on, just barely, so as not to make too much noise. Splashing a bit of ice-cold water on his face, and wiping it off, he looked in the mirror. A determined man looked back.

Luna didn't hear him leave. He went down to the desk and used the phone to order her some room service. The note she would find when they knocked would explain that he had gone back to the office. The doorman happily accepted the fin and said he would make sure she got in a cab safely.

The snow was still coming down and the wind was fierce. The gentle, almost pretty flakes that coated the grime of the city had been replaced with icy, biting snow, which was whipping down the street, stinging the faces of any who ventured out. It was only a block to the front of the familiar triangular Flatiron building, but Henry was glad when he got back inside. It was still pretty early, just past six, and he didn't hear anyone else milling about. Henry took the stairs.

He noticed the sound of his feet on the floor, and it reminded him of the previous night, but then he heard another sound. It was a sort of rustling. There was a light on in Bobby's office. Though he wasn't in the mood for the strange little man, he was curious what he was up toat such an early hour. Henry opened the door and walked in to the outer office. He was astonished.

Bobby heard the door and quickly scurried up to meet Henry. "Hey there old buddy, how's it going today? Did you see the paper?"

"Uhm," Henry stammered, as he looked around the room, "No."

"Well, it sounds like your old pal, the DA, had a little run in down the street. I wonder what he was doing in this part of town at that hour. It was right outside, he was mugged. The paper says it was some street kids. What do you think of that?"

"I don't know, Bobby," Henry said, having regained his composure. He didn't like being caught off guard, and the office had nearly knocked him to the floor. Everywhere he looked there were stacks and stacks of books, magazines and newspapers. He looked down at Bobby with his eager, helpful face and asked, "Do you have today's paper? I haven't seen it yet."

"Oh, ya, sure, boss. I got it right here, just a second." He scurried around a stack of books and past a table with books above and below it, and stopped by a stack of newspapers, which was about 7 feet high. He reached his hand into the stack, and with the deftness of a magician, swiftly pulled the paper out from near the bottom. Bobby was deceptively quick and, in what seemed like an unreasonable amount of time, was standing back in front of Henry. "Here you go; it is on the front page."

Henry took the paper and, sure enough, it was today's. He considered asking why it was so far down in the stack, but though his head was pounding, he was starting to think more clearly, and realized that if he asked Bobby about it, Bobby would likely answer...at length. He read the front page and it was just as Bobby had described, the DA had been mugged, but wasn't severely injured. Henry handed the paper back to Bobby, who ran back and somehow replaced it in the stack.

"Well I just stopped in to say hi, I have a lot to do, so take care," Henry said as he quickly left. The stale smell of Bobby's office was more than he could stomach at the moment, and he really just wanted to be alone and to think about his next move. The office was as he had left it. Henry hung his coat on the hook and sat down behind his desk. He leaned back, tipped his hat over his eyes, and put his feet up. He felt rough and worn out. A few minutes later he realized that he wasn't actually doing much thinking. Henry gave in to his own exhaustion, but just before he fell into a deep sleep, the memory of his dream from earlier danced across his brain, and he thought to himself how similar it had been to Bobby's office. He slept.

THIRTY SEVEN

The Call

The pounding on the door startled Henry, but when he realized that there was someone outside the office, he yelled, "Hey, stop your pounding, I'm coming." He swung his feet off the desk, stretching as he got up. His head was pounding now, even more so with the fellow at the door. He walked out into the outer office, wiped a hand over his face, and reached for the knob. He turned it, behind the door, found a very large man and a very short man.

"Hey there, Henry," greeted Bobby, in a voice that could be described as two parts friendly, one part excited, and three parts pest. Henry considered the possibility that he was having a nightmare, but then Bobby continued, "This is Vlad, he is from the old country, I am not sure which one, but his English isn't so good. He does a bang up job at fixing things. I brought him up to connect your phone into the switchboard system. It is included in the rent."

"Oh yes, well, nice to meet you," Henry said, opening the door for them to enter. He extended his hand. Vlad shook his hand firmly, and gave Henry a nod, then said, "Make phone work...das?"

"Yes, thanks." Henry walked over to the desk in the outer office and said, "There are two, the secretary's phone, and mine in the back." Henry pointed to his desk.

"Das," said Vlad, as he set his toolbox down by the first desk.

Bobby jumped into the conversation, which had been overtaken by an uncomfortable pause, "I figured you have been pretty busy. I know Vlad well; he keeps this place running, so I took it upon myself to ask him to take care of it for you. I figured it was the least I could do. I like to keep the tenants happy."

Henry was just starting to wake up. He looked at Bobby, wishing that he had called Vlad a little later in the day, but managed a feeble smile and a nod. Bobby interpreted this as a sign to keep talking.

"Yes, everyone here loves Vlad; he makes sure that the heat is always perfect. If a door swells in the summer, he will get if fixed right up, lickity split. He has been here as long as I can remember, and I have been here a long time. A good man that Vlad," Bobby said, slapping Vlad on the back.

Vlad looked up and said, "Bobby good man too!" He smiled and returned to his task at hand.

There was another bit of uncomfortable silence. It was uncomfortable for Bobby, because he had run out of things to say, which almost never happened. For Henry it was just a matter of having a splitting headache. Then Bobby started up again.

"Hey, you don't look so great, boss. You need something? Wait a minute I'll be right back." And Bobby flew out into the hallway and disappeared into his office.

Vlad stood up, grabbed his toolbox and just as he was about to go into Henry's office, turned around and said in remarkably good English, "Bobby is a good man. He means well. Nicest guy I have ever met. He will grow on you."

"I thought you didn't speak English?" Henry said, with a sly smile.

"I didn't twenty years ago, but now, not so bad. Don't tell Bobby, or I will never get any work done. Boy, can he talk." Vlad gave Henry a wink, and went in to work on the other phone.

Henry smiled. He liked Vlad.

The door from Bobby's office flew back open and Bobby scurried down the hall. He handed Henry a glass with water and two odd looking red and white plastic capsules.

"What are these?" Henry looked at the odd little things in his hand.

"They will help, trust me." Bobby smiled and was silent.

Henry had learned that the only thing worse than Bobby's constant chatter, was his deafening stone-faced silence. He was quite sure that whatever they were, he could trust Bobby, and they wouldn't do him any harm. So he threw them in his mouth and drank the water. If nothing else, Henry was thirsty, so the water was appreciated. "Thanks, Bobby."

Just then Vlad came out of the office and said, "Finished Boss." No sooner had he said it, than the phone rang. It startled Henry, but not Vlad, or Bobby for that matter.

"We will let you get that," Bobby said as he closed the door behind him.

Henry walked over to the secretary's desk, picked up the receiver, and cautiously said, "Henry Wood Detective Agency."

A female voice came over the line, "Yes, this is Betty with the DA's office. There was an incident last night, the DA would like you to come down to see him as soon as possible."

Henry had expected this, so he simply said, "I will be there this afternoon." He hung up the phone.

He picked it back up, got the switchboard, and told them his home number. He figured Luna would be home and, though she probably needed a couple of little red capsules too, would need to do him a favor. It was time to get back to solving her father's puzzles.

The operator came back on and said there hadn't been an answer and would he like her to try again. Henry said, "No, I will try again later," and hung up the receiver. He looked at his watch, expecting it to be well past noon. It wasn't. He had been asleep for 15 minutes when Bobby came knocking. He just shook his head and went back to his desk to think. The wheels were in motion; the plan had worked; now he needed to figure out the next clue.

Thirty Eight

Basic Clue

The DA's office only confirmed what Henry had suspected. As soon as he walked in, the song and dance, the tough talking, the promises, all had the foul stench of corruption. Though he couldn't prove it, Henry knew that Tommy 'The Knife's' friend in the department, or one of them at least, was Mr. McKinley.

Henry hadn't been sure how the DA had planned to make the journal 'disappear', but he knew that once it was in his hands, it wouldn't stay there for long. Henry couldn't take any satisfaction in knowing he had been right, but at least the heat would die down, and Luna could get back to a normal life. Without the threat of the journal, which was likely nothing but a pile of ashes now, Tommy would get back to his normal business of crime and mayhem.

The cold wind was nipping at Henry's ears, as he fumbled with his keys. He walked through the door and saw Luna sitting at the table with the tools from the closet, the ones which Henry believed held another clue. She had a pad of paper and a serious look on her face. Luna looked up only briefly, when Henry walked in the door, nearly tripping over her suitcase.

"Sorry about that. I was getting ready to head home, when I started to think about what all of this could mean."

"Any ideas?" Henry said as he hung his coat on the hook and tossed his hat onto the credenza.

"When you told us about the closet, I believed you, but it didn't sink in until today. Atter I got home, I didn't feel great, but I have imposed upon your kind hospitality enough already, so I got ready to leave. I packed, but I just couldn't get the thought of the closet out of my mind."

"I can't explain how it works, or who is sending me this stuff, but whoever it is; they seem to know where we need to be looking."

Henry grabbed a cup and poured himself some coffee and selected a cookie. Taking a small bite, he added, "I see you did some baking. It smells great in here."

"Thanks, baking helps me think." She flipped the pages of the pad back to the beginning. "I didn't know what each of these was called, so I went down to see if you had a book or something."

"Sorry, I don't, but I can tell you the names of each..." Henry was interrupted,

"You do now. I hope you don't mind, but I just had to take a peek into the closet. There were two books." She paused and pulled them out from under some other sheets of paper and handed them to Henry. "Both books, 'Mastering Hand Tool Techniques' and 'Basic Box Making', were, er will be...published in 2007!" She took a deep breath, "It is hard to believe."

Henry flipped them open and sure enough, Luna was right. "So it looks like you have been working that pencil pretty hard?"

"I looked up each tool." On the paper was neatly written Try Square, T Bevel, Marking Knife, Marking Gauge, Chisel,

Pencil, and a Saw. "The saw is odd though, as it doesn't look like any of the ones in the book."

Henry looked at it, and he agreed, he had never seen anything like it before.

Luna freshened up her cup of coffee, "I am afraid I don't know much about figuring out secret codes."

"I have to admit that I am not seeing a pattern either. Up until now, the clues have been pretty subtle, and I didn't understand them at first." Henry's voice sort of trailed off as he popped the last bit of cookie into his mouth.

After a long, comfortable silence, Luna said, "I really hate to impose...I was going to call a cab..."

"Henry smiled, let's go." He set the book on box making down on top of all of Luna's notes.

Henry and Luna didn't talk much on the ride back to her place. He was going to miss having her around; she was going to miss him too. When he pulled up to her house, he got the bag out of the back seat and walked her to the door. There was a stack of newspapers and she picked them up before unlocking the door. The house was cold, but she felt good being there. Henry looked around as a precaution. A precaution to what, he wasn't sure. It just felt like the thing to do.

"Do you mind if I use your phone? I want to check on Sylvia and Winston."

Luna smiled and took her bag upstairs.

The phone rang twice before the familiar and proper voice of Winston answered. Henry asked about Sylvia, and told Winston about the two books from the next century. At the mention of the two titles, Winston said, "Hmmm."

"Hmmm? Do you know what it means?" Henry asked hopefully.

"Have you seen today's paper?" Winston asked.

"Yes, but only briefly. Why?" Henry pulled the top paper off the stack that Luna had set on the table, and looked at the date. "Yes, I have it."

Winston explained, "I read the paper every day, and for as long as I can remember there has been a tiny little ad for 'Stowe It Forever' gifts. But today, there was a half page advertisement. It is on page 12."

Henry flipped to the ad, and then yelled to Luna who was still upstairs, "Hey Luna, what was the name of the author of the box book?"

She walked into the kitchen and said, "I think it was Doug Stowe."

Henry turned the paper around so she could see the advertisement.

Luna's eyes lit up. She clapped her hands together. "That is what we detectives call a clue!"

She was very cute. Henry chuckled, "Winston, you are a genius my man. Well done."

"Happy to help, sir."

Henry hung up the phone and tore the ad out of the paper. "I will check it out tomorrow."

Luna got a serious look on her face. "We will check it out tomorrow."

"I will pick you up at 8."

THIRTY NINE

Dinner At Tommy's

The DA arrived on time. He was hungry and had no idea what was in store for him. Tommy had invited Sal and the other guys who helped retrieve the journal, just to show there weren't any hard feelings. Mark McKinley still had a black eye and his ribs were pretty tender, but he was in fine spirits.

Tommy passed around some Cuban cigars, and they all talked about family and their jobs. Mark liked hanging out with Tommy and his ilk. It was exciting. He enjoyed their stories and they didn't mind sharing the details in front of him. Mark didn't think of himself as being a crooked DA, quite the opposite. His view was more philosophical. He couldn't stop the mob from running numbers, gambling, selling liquor, and extortion, but he could keep it in check. It worked out well for Tommy, too. He could schedule a time and place for when a bust was going to go down, which cut down on his guys getting killed. They did a few years in prison, some even got off, and then they would get their 'time off' bonus, as he liked to call it.

The city was big enough that Mark got plenty of murder convictions without needing to go after Tommy's men. Since it was widely known among the criminal element that Tommy's boys had a fair amount of leeway, when it came to torture and killing, it meant that people were more cooperative and thus, less killing was needed. That is, until the other families started to make a play for Manhattan.

Tommy raised his glass, "To my friend Mark, who has put an end to the bloodshed with his courageous act."

"Salud." They raised their glasses and smiled.

Tommy, "I just wanted to show my appreciation for helping put an end to all of the fighting. To think, the other families would try to take advantage of rumors of a journal, which would show me as criminal, well it is disappointing."

They all agreed that Tommy was a fine upstanding citizen who was greatly misunderstood. Tommy smiled and looked at Mark, "Sal tells me you can really take a punch."

"I think your boys eased up a little," Mark said, being modest. His ribs were killing him.

"I didn't," said one of the thugs at the table. Everyone laughed and the thug slapped the DA on the back. "You take a punch real good, Mr. District Attorney."

Dinner was served, and the good cheer and laughter continued. When the plates were cleared away, the staff closed the doors, and it got very quiet. Mark tried to make a joke but nobody smiled. Tommy just stared at him.

"What's going on fellas?" Mark said, the nervousness apparent. Tommy stood up and walked around the table to the sideboard and removed the journal. "I have a few concerns, Mr. McKinley." He dropped the journal on the table with a thwack. "I think you gave me a fake."

"No I didn't, swear to God. I took it from Henry's office and then straight to your guys. When would I have had time to copy it?"

"I didn't say copy, I said fake."

"I don't understand. What's the difference? It doesn't matter--I gave you the journal I got from the detective."

"Maybe, you made this fake ahead of time and kept the real one? Maybe, you think you want to renegotiate our terms?"

Mark went white when Tommy pulled the tire iron out of the drawer, "I want you to look at it." Mark did as he was told. He flipped through a couple of pages and then the expression on his face changed. He held a page up to the light, then another. He went to the back page and checked it, too.

Then he stood up and went to the lamp on the credenza and looked again.

Tommy wasn't the smartest guy in the world, but he could tell that it wasn't an act. Sal saw it, too and asked, "What do you have to say for yourself?"

Mark didn't look as frightened anymore, "You are right, it's a fake. I worked a forgery case when I was the ADA. We had an expert on the stand who testified to being tipped off by the uniformity of each page. The pressure of the numbers and letters is the same throughout the entire journal. No matter how precise a person is, they don't always write exactly the same way, over many weeks or months. This was done in a matter of days or hours."

"So who made it?"

"I don't have any idea, but supposedly Henry had it for a while, so I am thinking he made the copy."

"How do you know it is a copy and not just a bunch of random numbers?"

"I can't say for sure, but it is slower to make up stuff than to simply copy it. My guess is, he kept the original."

Tommy put the tire iron back in the drawer. "You are a smart man, too smart to try to pull something like this."

Sal and the others nodded. The color returned to Mark's face and Sal poured him another drink.

Tommy told everyone to enjoy themselves; he was going to go consider his options.

FORTY

Francis At Restaurant

Francis sat at the restaurant thinking about Mike and unable to enjoy the meal. It was a rare day when idle thoughts would be able to distract him from eating. He planned on going back to the hospital after he finished the article, but at the rate he was going, that might be a while.

He opened his notebook and took a bite of the food. It was quite good, not overcooked, and the presentation was nice. The atmosphere was pleasant, though at this time of day, it was hard to tell. Francis preferred to eat at the height of the dinner rush. He would judge the food, not only by using his palate, but by watching the faces of other patrons. In New York, people weren't shy, if they didn't like something, they sent it back. This was his secret to reviewing. Any chef, worth his weight in truffles, could put together something brilliant for one man eating alone with a pencil and notebook. Could he do it for all of the people at the restaurant? That was the question he strived to answer.

When Francis gave a restaurant his seal of approval it would send people flocking to their tables, but if he were wrong, then people would blame him. Francis fooled around with his salad and noticed a very worried chef watching from the back. The chef's name was Rolando, he was 23 and this would be his first major review. Since the restaurant was empty, being after the lunch rush and before the dinner crowd, Francis decided to give him a break and explain.

To the waitress, "Could you please ask Rolando, if he might have a minute, to join me?"

"Yes sir."

Rolando tried to pace his walk, but he looked like he wanted to run. Or maybe it was his legs threatening give out. Francis wasn't sure. When he arrived at the table, Francis stood and shook his hand.

"I wanted to talk to you."

"Yes, Mr. Le Mange, it is an honor to meet you."

"I assure you the pleasure is mine. Please sit."

Now, most of the staff was nervously looking on, too.

"I don't make it a habit of speaking with the chefs and do my best to remain anonymous, but today is not like most days."

"Oh, how so?" Rolando said, seeing the pain on the critics face.

"My mind isn't on the food. It is elsewhere and I have been sitting here picking at it. I noticed you had observed such, and I wanted to make it clear, it wasn't the food's fault."

"You seem troubled, sir; may I ask what is weighing so heavily on your mind?"

Francis liked him. He spoke well and carried himself with a grace normally reserved for much older men. He was not brash, as the young so often are, he was kind. "A dear friend is in the hospital and my thoughts are with him."

"I am sorry to hear your friend is sick."

"Thank you, but he isn't sick. He was beaten by a gang of thugs. He is a policeman."

"Is it the man in the paper?"

"Yes."

They sat in silence for a moment, until Francis asked, "When did you first start to cook?"

"I was four years old and helped my mother back in Spain. I would wash the vegetables and get her pots and pans. She called me her little sous chef. I honestly can't remember doing anything else."

Francis found this to be fascinating. He knew plenty of chefs, but this one had a story and an interesting one, at that. "When did you come to America?"

"In 1938 my family moved from Spain. My father smelled the coming trouble and said it was time to go. His brother had come over in 1935 and drove a cab. My uncle loved being a cabbie and convinced my father to buy their own medallion and go into business. They now have 37 cabs and do very well. My uncle and father put up the money and helped me start the restaurant."

Francis sat there listening as he ate. The food really was special. The waitress brought Rolando a cup of coffee, and the young chef continued to tell his story. They talked for close to an hour. Francis finished his meal and even had some dessert.

Francis thanked Rolando for his company and the fine meal. In the cab, riding back to the paper, he realized he felt much better. It took very little time for him to write his review. It wasn't a typical review as he devoted more inches to the man than the food.

FORTY ONE

Rule 4

Henry couldn't see the endgame. It ate at him like a parasite. This case, the only one he had been working for weeks, was gnawing at his soul. He felt the end was near, that the final pieces to the puzzle were about to be handed to him. And then what?

Big Mike was recovering, but still in the hospital. Luna and Sylvia had their fathers in the wind, and he knew they would stay there until Tommy and the DA were safely behind bars. Life didn't always deal you a good hand, and Henry thought his cards were dreadful. He did have an ace in the hole, and he hoped that would be enough.

He got up from the kitchen table and started to pace. Tomorrow he would drive over and pick up Luna to go poking around 'Stowe It Forever' gifts. It was painfully obvious that every step needed to be clear in his mind. Henry picked up the book from 2007, 'Basic Box Making' and flipped through the pages for the 10th time. He wasn't sure what the key would be, but it had to be in the book, so he did his best to understand everything he could about box making.

Henry thought to himself, "When this is over, I need to make some of these boxes." Then he shook his head, he was getting distracted. He had compiled a list of steps and was not thrilled that it was a list of one. He was much more comfortable being able to see 3, 4 or 5 moves ahead. This wasn't a game of chess, though he liked the metaphor. It was a deadly game, being played with the lives of people, with which, he had developed a bond.

Henry chastised himself for caring. The 3rd rule of being a private detective, "Don't get too close to the client." Rule one was to not negotiate on fees, and rule two had something to do with domestic abuse cases. He couldn't remember rule two very well, it wasn't his own, but was passed down to him by his mentor, Mickey. He shook himself again, as rule four leapt out and smacked him across the face, "Always stay focused."

Rule four was killing him. *Ok, Henry, stop worrying about finding the rest of the code to decipher the journal. It will be there, you will figure it out, no matter how difficult or subtle the clue might be.* It wasn't a rule, but Henry believed that self-confidence was important. Perhaps he would make it rule 2, since he never remembered it anyway? His internal voice continued, *Assuming we find the rest of the key, or some of it, what is the play?*

Rule four continued to take a beating as Henry started to nibble on one of the cookies Luna had left. She really knew her way around the kitchen. He was sure that there must be some sort of clause, for rule four, which allowed for a temporary loss of focus in the event of an emergency snack. Some more pacing, while the cookies continued to disappear along with the milk. He couldn't bring the future into focus no matter how hard he tried. All his thoughts were spinning like a bunch of lights at a carnival.

Outside the wind was up and starting to bang on the neighborhood. It would have sounded worrisome, to Henry, but he couldn't hear a thing. His mind was lost in the case. Three cookies and a glass of milk later and he had the book back in his hand. What would he need to find, where would the next piece be hidden? He imagined there would be something in a box, but he wondered, if that was too simple. Maybe there would be a bookshelf, perhaps made by Stowe, which would have the clue? He stopped pacing and laid down on the couch. He put his arm over his eyes, and while he tried to follow rule four, drifted off to sleep.

FORTY TWO

Message In A Box

The night before had brought a storm down on the neighborhood with an unforgiving wrath. There were trees down, his power was out, and the phone lines were dead. He took a cold shower. Henry didn't feel much like eating, so he fumbled around in the early morning dark, found his keys, and stood at the door looking out into the bleak winter day.

Luna was expecting him at 8 am. Normally he wouldn't have left for another hour, but the mayhem of the previous night's storm added some uncertainty to his travel time. He pulled on his overcoat, grabbed his hat and gloves, and opened the front door, hoping this would be the day he could put all the pieces together.

Several downed trees forced a circuitous route out of the neighborhood. Henry wondered what would happen to the trees. He hadn't had much time for woodworking of late, and the fallen lumber reminded him of that fact. He hoped they would be sawed up and turned into something useful. He drove on. Thirty minutes later the sun decided to join him on the drive. The sky looked to be clearing up, and road crews seemed to have a good handle on clearing up the mess.

He arrived at Luna's place with two minutes to spare. Promptness made Henry happy, especially when he did so under such circumstances, with so many unknown variables.

Luna hopped in the car, her hands wrapped around a basket with a gingham cloth draped over it.

"I didn't know if you would bother with breakfast, so I brought these," Luna said, as she lifted the red checked cloth. A wave of blueberry muffin goodness immediately filled the car. Henry smiled, with his usually calm demeanor, while his stomach was giving thanks.

He accepted the proffered muffin and took a bite, chewed it slowly, took another, and forgot about projecting his normal 'tough guy image', as he made what could only be described as, a purring noise.

"Do you like them?" Luna asked knowingly.

Henry offered more purring with a hint of deep guttural grunting of approval. Henry could take a punch and keep his cool, but he was powerless against baked goods. He was sure that this day was on the right track.

They drove along in silence for a while, as both of them enjoyed the muffins. Before Henry asked for thirds, he thought it best to discuss their plan. "I have been thinking about what we should keep our eyes open for. It could be anything. If nothing jumps out at me, and I am sure it won't, I may need to poke around more than the shopkeeper would like."

"It could be anywhere, in a drawer, under something..." Luna said while staring off at the road ahead.

"Yes. I may need you to distract him with your feminine charms," Henry said with an air of authority, as if he were talking to the troops before they stormed the castle.

"My feminine charms you say? I didn't think you noticed," Luna said, looking at him as she offered him another muffin.

Henry felt like a blush might be coming on, so he took a muffin, in part to hide from Luna, and the fact that she had knocked him off his game. Luna wasn't fooled.

Henry ate the muffin and seemed to focus more intently than ever on the road ahead. Luna wrapped up the basket and folded her arms across it. She decided to have mercy on him and changed to a more serious tone.

"Do you think we will solve the code and be able to put an end to all of this? I miss my father," she said in a low, now sad voice.

"I know we will." Henry said, with confidence, though he had his doubts. He had a nagging fear that they might not find the next clue, that this trip was just a snipe hunt. Without the code to the journal, which 'Tommy the Knife' was under the impression had been destroyed, they would be out of luck. As in chess, today's move would be pivotal, one misstep and all would be lost.

They drove past 'Stowe It Forever' gift shop, the one from the ad, and Henry checked his mirror. Nobody had been following them. Everything had calmed down since the DA's visit and the subsequent 'journal' incident, but he still favored caution; once more around the block, just to make sure. He parked the car. They walked slowly to the shop. Luna took his arm to help keep her footing on the icy sidewalk. Henry reminded her, "Now it is going to be tough. I don't know what we are looking for, and I have no idea how we will find it."

A little bell over the door announced their presence and a tiny man with a monocle, scurried from behind a curtain leading to the back room. The shop was filled to the brim with boxes, cases, clocks, furniture, steamer trunks, lamps and possibly lost pirate treasure. Henry whispered, "Oh God, this might take a while." Luna squeezed his arm in agreement, as she greeted the tiny man behind the counter.

"Hello there, my name is Luna and this is my...friend...Henry," she said.

"Excellent, it is good to meet you. I am Wolfgang the manager," he said with a slight German accent and a familiarity that struck them both as odd. He spoke in short fast bursts with gaps too small to allow Henry or Luna to sneak in a word. "Wait right here..." And off he went, though he continued to talk, "quite a storm last night....power just came back on..." There was a rustling sound, then a loud wooden sound of a drawer being opened and closed, then another. This went on for a couple of minutes, as did his ramblings.

Wolfgang reappeared behind the counter with a tiny box. There was a small, retecangular, red velvet, mat on the counter, and he placed it in the center. "This is what you have come for. I have, as instructed, not opened it. It is paid for. I hope you enjoy it for many years to come. Good day." He disappeared behind the curtain.

Henry and Luna looked at each other blankly. Henry looked at the tiny box, then at Luna. There wasn't anyone else in the shop. Luna reached over and took off the lid. Inside there was a tiny folded piece of white paper.

Luna and Henry walked back to the car in silence, Luna holding the tiny box firmly in both hands. Henry broke the silence as he put his key in the door, to unlock it. "That went well, though not at all as I had expected." He opened the passenger door, and Luna slid into the car with just a nod. The sound of the door closing, and the silence that followed Henry back around the car, reminded him that Luna was holding a message from her father. He thought about the fear she had been living with since the day he went missing, and how she had maintained her wits throughout it all. She was a tough cookie. He got in the car and started it up.

They drove for a little while, again in silence. Luna said in a quiet voice, "Should I open it?"

"Yes," Henry said, keeping his eyes on the road.

Luna took off the lid and set it in her lap. She opened the piece of paper and then read it aloud.

Dear Luna,

I hope this message finds you well. We are doing fine, but miss our girls. Please tell Sylvia and Winston that her father is safe. He feels terrible about what he put her through, but apologies will have to wait for later. I hope that this codex, the list of names, and the journal will be enough to put the people who would harm us, behind bars.

Love,
Dad

"The rest is the remainder of the codex," she said with a sigh. "It isn't dated, so I don't know when he left this for us, but I do feel a little better."

Henry smiled at her. "Yes, I do too. Now that we can decipher the journal, we will know what Tommy 'The Knife' has been up to, and why your father had to disappear."

"It is a good thing we made that copy to give to the DA. I thought you were crazy at the time, but it looks like you were right about him, "she said, returning the message to the tiny box.

"Yes, I can smell a rat. And the stink on him is almost overwhelming."

There wasn't much more to say. Henry drove and Luna rapped her fingers on the lid of the box. She was thinking about her father, wondering where he was, and Henry was forming his plan. He would need to get some help. He would need a bit of luck.

FORTY THREE

Mike Comes Home

Mike had been a pretty good patient. Of course, he had been on a lot of pain meds, which helped. When it was time to leave, he was ready to run out of the hospital. They made him sit in a wheel chair while a frightening woman, with sizable girth, pushed him. Francis was by his side, smirking. It didn't go unnoticed.

Francis pulled up his car and Mike got in. Their perceptions of one another had changed and both had a new friend. Mike, not a sentimentalist said, "I appreciate the ride."

"You are welcome."

The car pulled out and Mike said, "You mind swinging by the precinct?"

"I was given strict orders, by Sally Mae, to bring you straight home."

Mike laughed. "She is a handful, that is sure. She had the entire staff on their best behavior. I wouldn't be surprised if she was approving purchasing and scheduling the operating room."

"Everyone was powerless against her angry face."

Mike shook his head, "I know, it was something to watch. One of the doctors had said he would check on me at 8:00. At one minute after eight, she went to find him. I heard them coming five minutes later, she was giving him an earful all the way down the hall. He checked me out, while she glared at him, with her arms crossed. All I could think was how the detectives down at the precinct could use her in the interrogation room."

Francis loved that story. He had been trying to write a novel. It hadn't gone well, so he was looking for inspiration wherever he could find it. "She is a fireball, that one. Was the doctor ever late again?"

"He was not."

Francis turned to the right and headed towards the precinct. "You will make it quick. I don't want to incur Sally Mae's wrath."

"I just want to see the captain. Five minutes tops."

Francis waited in the car while Mike went inside. The squad room was mostly empty, but a few guys saw Mike and welcomed him back. He knocked on the captain's door, and then went in. "Cap, you got a few minutes?"

The captain stood up and walked around to shake Mike's hand. "Good to see you, Mike."

After the pleasantries, "Captain I know I am not going to be out on the beat for a while, but I will go crazy if I don't have something to do. I'd like to work on my case, read the file, see if I can help."

"You know I can't do that. If I did, we couldn't use you as a witness."

Mike knew he was right, "But captain, I have to do something. I can't stand being out of the game."

The captain sat back down, "Well, now that you mention it, I do have something."

"I'll take it."

"You don't know what it is."

"I don't care, even paperwork, just something."

"You hate that crap."

"I hate it, because I want to be out on the streets, but right now, I couldn't chase down a one legged thief, so I'll do it."

"Well, it isn't paperwork. You've been reading the papers, you know what it has been like. The gangs are shooting each other up and we are stacking bodies in the morgue like cord wood. The problem is the detectives are overworked, the cases keep coming in, and nothing is getting closed. The other problem is that a lot of the guys in the morgue are suspected of other murders. There are families waiting for us to catch their loved one's killers, to put those cases to bed, and I fear that their cases will go cold and they will never get their answers. I had this put together," he walked over to a box with a couple of dozen files in it. "These are not the complete case files, but summaries. There is also a list of all the guys who have been taken out recently. I need you to go through everything and try to get a the big picture. I fear there are a lot of connections, which can't be seen, because they are being worked on by different detectives."

"I'm not a detective, but I can read. I am glad to do it."

"It is quite a mess. You may not thank me once you dig into the pile, but it will keep you busy."

Mike picked up the box with his good arm and left with a smile. He couldn't wait to get home and start being a cop again.

Francis pulled up in front of Mike's place and grabbed the box from the back seat. Mike smiled at the 'Welcome Home Mike' sign. The sign, written in crayon with lots of signatures, and a big printed Sally Mae, was perfect. The curtains moved, the front door opened, Sally Mae ran out and hugged Mike.

The house was full of friends from the department and neighborhood. On the table were cakes, casseroles, pasta, and lots of cookies. Mike, generally a private person, wasn't used to crowds gathered in his honor, but didn't seem to mind. Sally Mae took his hand and showed him the table of food, then took his coat.

"We are putting the coats on the bed. I am working the door. You have fun, but don't overdo."

Mike asked, "Did you plan my party?"

"I did, but the neighborhood helped. Everyone brought food and signed the banner. I was in charge, so just told people what needed to be done."

Mike made the rounds and though everyone wanted to ask how he was doing, he was more interested in hearing about what they had been up to. It was good to be out of the hospital. They talked about the weather and the coming baseball season, and he felt good.

Forty Four

Charred

"I miss him," Luna said, holding the tiny box on her lap. The note inside had been simple. It explained how to apply the codex to the journal and decipher it. She had read the note to Henry once, and then again, to herself. Afterwards, she folded the note and put it back in the box.

"It isn't safe for your father, or for Sylvia's, until Tommy 'The Knife' and the DA are behind bars," Henry said solemnly.

"I know. Do you have a plan?" she said, softly.

Henry didn't answer, but gave a nod. The car got quiet again. He had a hint of a plan, but it wasn't clear exactly how to make it work. His decision to make a copy of the original journal and give it to the DA, was a good one, and he knew it. The reasoning was sound. If the DA was dirty, as he suspected, then the copy would get destroyed or turned over to Tommy. If the DA had been on the up and up, then it wouldn't have mattered, as Henry still needed to find the rest of the codex. Either way, he figured the move would get the heat off Luna. It had worked.

Now, he had it. He was sure the first move would be to go over the journal. Henry hoped there would be something in it, tying the DA to Tommy. If there wasn't, it was going to be considerably more difficult to reel in both of them. Henry explained his plan to Luna; she smiled and gave a slight nod.

They decided it would be quickest if they went to Sylvia's house, and everyone could work on the journal decoding together. Henry drove with a sense of urgency. This case had been going on for too long. It needed to come to an end. He needed to finish it.

The thickness of the forest hid the smoke. When the car rounded the last curve, Luna gasped. Sylvia's house was but a shell. The charred walls smoldered, the snow around was gone and there was a gray ashen muck radiating out from the once beautiful home. Henry slowed the car down and finally stopped. He looked at Luna and said, "Stay here!"

She took her hand off the door handle and put it back onto the tiny box. She looked frightened. Henry pulled his revolver out from the glove box and opened the door. He stepped out of the car onto the wet gray muck and gave Luna one more look. She understood and had no intention of getting out of the car.

He walked up to where the front door had been, pushed his way through, and stood in the entry way. He looked up and could see the sky where there should be a second floor. Henry pulled back the hammer on the gun. The click of the revolver seemed louder than Henry had remembered. All around it was unnaturally quiet.

He walked towards the hallway, which led to the study. Then he saw something familiar, something awful. He rushed up and leaned over the crumpled body of Winston. He gently rolled him over and Winston gave a little gasp.

"What happened?" Henry said holding Winston.

He took a pained breath, and then coughed, and blood trickled out of the corner of his mouth. "Tommy and his thugs came and took Sylvia. I tried not to..." Winston coughed some more and his body shuddered.

"Stay with me, we are going to get you to the hospital, they will fix you up..." Henry lied.

"I let you down sir," Winston said shaking.

"You have been great. Where did they take Sylvia?" Henry asked, sensing that there wasn't much time.

"I don't know. I don't know. I tried not to tell, but Tommy had a gun to her head, he said she was dead if I didn't talk," Winston said softly, fading, and then added, "They know about the copy."

"Hang in there buddy," Henry said, as he felt Winston let go. It wasn't the first time Henry had seen death; a short prayer and a few seconds of holding onto the feeling, so he wouldn't ever forget, and Henry was back in the present. He found a sheet, in a closet which was only partly burned, and placed it over Winston.

It is strange how, in the gray muck, at the moment that Winston's life slipped away, the fog in Henry's mind, surrounding the end game, lifted. Henry walked out to the car. Luna had stayed in the front seat, clinging to the tiny box. When he told her, she hung her head, sobbed and pulled the tiny box to her chest.

Henry had to see Big Mike.

FORTY FIVE

The Next Move

Henry pulled the car out from the drive and made a left onto the main road. He still had the smell of wet, charred, murder and arson, burning his nostrils. Luna wept to herself. They drove, in silence, for about 5 minutes and pulled into the first gas station he saw. The attendant, an old man with an oil stained rag in his back pocket, came out to meet him.

"Hey there old timer, you got a phone?" Henry said.

"Sure, but it's for customers. You buying any gas?"

Henry handed the man three bucks and went in to use the phone. His first call was to the fire department. Nobody had noticed the fire before he and Luna had gotten there, or they would have been on the scene.

He then picked up the phone and called the hospital. They told him Mike had gone home that morning. Henry looked out front; the old man was cleaning the windows, and eyeing Luna. Henry made one more call. "Hey, Mike," he said, when he heard a voice on the other end.

"No, this is Joe, Mike is in the kitchen. Who is this?"

"It's Henry Wood; you mind putting him on...it's important."

"Sure, I'll get him."

Henry heard the phone being set down, and from the sound of the room, Mike must have gotten a welcome home party. A few moments later he heard someone hobbling towards the phone, "Henry, how is it going?" said Mike in a familiar and booming voice.

"Not so good, my friend, but before I get to that, how are you doing?"

"I am on the mend. Still got the arm in a sling, but the bruising has gone down, the headaches have stopped, and I am itching to get back on the beat. They tell me I have to rest for two more weeks."

"I am glad to hear it, buddy," Henry said, with a bit of relief in his voice. He needed some good news and this made Henry feel a little better about bothering Mike.

"Thanks....now tell me what is up?" Mike said, while lowering his voice and changing to a serious tone.

"I need to see you. I need to see you now. May I come over?"

"Sure thing Henry, we can talk in the back, if it needs to be private," Mike said.

"Thanks...on my way," Henry said and hung up the phone.

He returned to the car and thanked the old man. Henry took Luna's hand as he pulled out of the station. "Don't worry. I have a plan."

She squeezed his hand and smiled. She had stopped crying and was trying to steady herself. The rest of the drive to Big Mike's house passed without a word between them.

Forty Six

Getting Mike's Help

The street was packed with parked cars, there were two people standing outside smoking and talking. A car was just leaving, so Henry took the spot. "Luna, I need to talk to Mike. I am going to ask him to keep an eye on you..."

Luna immediately flashed a look at Henry and objected, "I am coming with you!"

"No you aren't! You are going to stay here, and stay out of it. I am going to get Sylvia and put an end to this, once and for all," Henry said in a calm measured tone, with a cold forcefulness which left no question as to who was in charge. Luna affixed a look of anger to her face, but her eyes revealed relief. She did make Henry walk around and open the door for her, however, and walked with heavy pouting steps, on their way to Mike's front door.

In Luna's mind, she could see herself behaving like a small child, and she didn't like it, but her emotions were so mixed up, she didn't know what to do. She knew that Henry was about to risk his life, for Sylvia, and for her father, and sitting in the car sobbing, seemed ungrateful. Though in truth, she really wanted to hide, to go back to the way life was, to forget that all of this ever happened.

Henry knocked on the door; Sally Mae opened up and said, in a grown up voice, "Hello Henry, good to see you." Her eyes were bright; she wore a little pink dress and had bows in her hair. She had worried and cared for Mike, as much as any doctor or nurse at the hospital. Now it appeared she was helping with the welcome home party.

"Hello Sally Mae. You look quite lovely in your pink dress today," Henry said with a smile.

She beamed, was a kid again and quickly replied, "It's new, just for today. I helped make the cake too!" She stepped back and pointed to the table in front of a big sign which read, 'We Love You Big Mike'. There were people everywhere, with plates of food, talking and laughing. Sally Mae said, back in her grown up voice, "There is food, and punch, and of course cake. May I take your hat and your coats?"

Luna couldn't help herself; a smile snuck onto her face, and a little bit of joy found its way into her weary heart. "Thank you, Sally Mae." She took off her coat and handed it to her. Henry did the same and then plopped his hat on top of her head. She giggled and ran off to the back bedroom. Henry noticed Mike talking with Francis across the room.

Mike saw Henry and gave a nod. He made his way through the people, shook Henry's hand with his left hand, and gave a smile to Luna. She smiled back, feeling suddenly shy. Henry lowered his voice, "Is there someplace we can talk?"

Mike continued to thank people for the party as he and Henry made their way to his little office in the back of the house. It was cluttered with lots of books, newspapers, magazines, and general guy chaos. Mike leaned up against his desk, "What's going on Henry?" Henry closed the door, took a moment to think about what he was going to ask, and then started to catch Mike up.

"It's a mess, Mike. They took Sylvia, and gave Winston the same treatment they gave you, but he won't be getting any welcome home parties."

Mike's face turned to stone. "Go on."

Henry went back to the day Mike had been beaten up. He went over every detail, explaining how they had made a copy, which they had given to the DA, how the DA was in it up to his eyes, and how Henry thought it had to play out. Mike listened, getting angrier as each new revelation was made.

Henry laid out every detail, and then he let Mike digest it. Overwhelmed, he paced back and forth, talking to himself and Henry. "I didn't want to believe that someone on the force could be in cahoots with Tommy 'The Knife', but if the DA is crooked, we can't trust anybody." Henry had reached the same conclusion and could see the moment of realization in Mike's eyes. There was silence for a long while, as they both let the truth of the situation sink in.

Mike agreed to make a few calls, and to watch over Luna while Henry went after Sylvia. A little knock at the door and a tiny voice let them know the meeting was over. Sally Mae asked if Big Mike was getting tired and should maybe lie down for a bit of a rest. Mike chuckled, told her he was fine, and they were coming back to the party right away.

Henry talked with Francis for a bit, shook a few hands, and then said goodbye to Luna. He found his coat and hat and then headed out. He bummed a cigarette from one of the guys smoking outside, and slowly walked back to his car. He knew the next call would be the when and where. There was nothing to do but wait.

FORTY SEVEN

Captured

Sylvia sat in a dark room tied to a chair. She had a bruise on her arm, where one of the thugs had grabbed her. Her mind was all over the place. She worried about Winston. She thought about her father and Luna. Would they try to grab her too? She didn't think so because Luna was with Henry.

Fear and worry gave way to anger; anger at her father for his stupid inventions, for changing her life, and then running off. Why did he have to do all of this cloak and dagger stuff? To protect her, huh, it didn't work too well did it? She struggled against the ropes, and they bit into her wrists. Why didn't they just leave the gangsters alone? It was up to the police to catch the bad guys, not an old inventor and accountant. Exhaustion shoved the other emotions aside, as sadness settled in for the night. Sylvia knew he loved her and she loved him for the man he was, for his belief in right and wrong. She could see it was brave, and he did arrange for Henry to help.

A noise from outside brought her back to the moment. It sounds of people arriving terrified her. They were keeping their voices down and she couldn't tell what was being said. There was something about a call which had been made. Obviously, she was the bait to get the journal back. Henry's plan hadn't worked at all. Now she was mad at him, too.

The door opened and a large man walked in and asked, "How you doing Miss?"

She wanted to act tough, but it seemed pointless. These guys really were tough, and it would likely just make him laugh. "I am scared and..." She looked at the floor.

He sort of felt bad for her. She was a good looking broad and if she started crying, well, he didn't want to think about that. "And what? It's okay, you hungry?"

She was, "Well yes, but I need to, um, do you have a bathroom?"

Shit, he thought, she had been tied up for hours. "Sure, I'll untie you." He considered telling her no funny business, but she seemed too scared to run, so he untied her and said, "Follow me."

They walked out into the other room. Some of the guys stood and took off their hats, two of them didn't look at her, and the others just stared blankly. They didn't like doing this to a broad. It wasn't how things were done. None of them were happy about it.

He pointed to the bathroom door and then told one of the guys to run to the deli and get some sandwiches and Cokes. The guy looked relieved to be doing something, and one of his buddies volunteered to go with him.

They heard her washing her hands and then she walked out. This time they all stood up. She walked back to the room, and he followed her. She sat down and rubbed her wrists. They were red from the ropes. She waited for him to tie her up again, but he didn't.

"A couple of the boys went out for sandwiches and Cokes. They won't be long. I don't think we need to tie you up again."

"Thanks. It sort of hurts."

He just shrugged, not feeling very tough, doing this to a woman and all.

"Are you going to kill me?"

He wanted to say no, but he had no idea what Tommy was thinking. He wanted to reassure her, but it was too late, that moment had passed.

Sylvia looked at the floor, not feeling very hungry anymore. She felt like crying, but had done plenty of that, and wasn't sure there were any tears left.

There wasn't much in the room. The brick walls had some cobwebs, and the windows were blacked out. The wood floors were covered in a thin layer of dust. It was warm though.

The silence was starting to bother Sal. He considered going back into the other room, but that didn't feel right. He wanted to say something to make her feel better, but instead said, "You think this Henry guy will come through?"

"You mean rescue me?"

"No, I mean, bring the journal."

"Does it really matter if he does?"

"It might. Tommy can be unpredictable."

"You mean unpredictable in a good way?" Sylvia asked without really believing it could be true.

He let out a heavy sigh, "Not usually, no."

She smiled. His honesty somehow made her feel better. She thought about truth and why knowing it was important. An answer didn't come to mind, so she asked him, "Thanks for not bull shitting me."

He looked at her, confused by her smile. He didn't feel like smiling, but did anyway.

She asked, "What's your name?"

Telling a kidnap victim your name seemed like a bad idea. He hated it when his men did stupid things like that. "It's Salvatore Miss."

She couldn't help but be polite, "Well I am Sylvia, it is..." She paused and added awkwardly, "...much appreciated, your kindness, that is."

He didn't feel kind. Sal wasn't good at small talk. "You like books? I could get you something to read."

"Yes, I like books, but I doubt I could start something I wouldn't be able to finish. Thanks though."

Sal felt like a complete heel now. What a terrible thing to ask someone in her spot. He wished the food would get here, so he could put something, other than his foot, in his mouth. The silence was back, and he felt trapped. Sal didn't feel in control, though he was. He hadn't felt this way since 'The Kids' funeral. She seemed like a really nice lady. He guessed she was smart, because of how she talked. He imagined she did like books, maybe some of the same books he liked. He stopped trying to say the right thing.

"Yeah, I guess that was a stupid thing for me to ask. Sorry."

The apology from this giant of a man touched Sylvia. She could tell he would let her go, if it were up to him. It wasn't, and she understood. "It is okay, you were just being considerate. Do you like to read?"

The nicer she got, the worse he felt. "Yes," he lowered his voice a bit, "Most of the guys in my line of work, aren't really into the classics. I don't know why. We spend a lot of time in cars waiting for things to happen. I usually have a book with me. The guys probably would give me a hard time, if I weren't so big."

She laughed, "Yes, I bet they would. But it is because they don't know how enjoyable a good book can be. I like mysteries and love stories."

"Did you know that Edgar Allen Poe wrote the first mystery?"

Her captor was full of surprises. "No, I didn't."

"I read it a long time ago. I like his stuff, even the poem 'The Raven'."

"You like poetry, too?"

"Not really that much, but 'The Raven' was in a book with his other stuff, so I read it. He makes you feel like you are in the room watching the guy deal with his demons and insecurities." Sylvia's expression was easy to read, Sal continued, "My day job is being a thug, by night, I am a secret literary critic, saving people from poor prose."

Sylvia giggled. She hadn't forgotten where they were or why, or what was next, but it was how she felt.

FORTY EIGHT

Two Calls

Henry walked slowly up the stairs. The weight of this case was nearly unbearable. His head was pounding, but the die was cast, and soon there would be a resolution, for good or bad. Each step rang hollow in the hallway and seemed to echo into eternity. The rest of the world was silent.

When he neared the door of the strange little man, his landlord Bobby, he found himself trying to quiet his steps. It wasn't intentional, nor did it matter. He heard the patter of Bobby's feet and the door opened, though with less flair than usual.

"Hey Henry..." Bobby said, and then lowered his voice a bit and slowed his pace, "How you doin? Anything you need?"

"No Bobby, but thanks for asking," Henry said, and smiled. The shortness of the meeting seemed odd, but he was thankful, he didn't feel like getting into one of Bobby's long winded discussions. Bobby turned and went back into his horribly cluttered office and shut the door gently.

The Henry Wood Detective Agency seemed cold, but when he checked the thermostat, it was fine. He took off his hat and coat, put them on the hat tree and sat down at the desk. He leaned slowly back, keeping his gaze on the phone, eyeing it suspiciously, like it might bite him. He waited.

The phone rang. It sounded strange somehow. It rang again and Henry leaned forward and slowly picked up the receiver. He didn't say anything.

"Mr. Wood, I presume," said the voice on the other end.

"Yes. Who is this?" Henry said with a sudden confidence and swagger that may have been posturing, but it felt right. The game was on.

"This is the man, whose business you and your little friends, have been sticking your noses into."

"I have a lot of cases. Could you be more specific?" Henry responded as if he didn't have a care in the world.

Tommy's short fuse had been lit and he roared into the phone, "Listen you little bastard. I have your broad Sylvia, you have my book. You are going to bring me the book, and I won't burn your world to the ground."

"You are a scum bag. I doubt Sylvia is still alive. If she is, we can work something out," Henry said, thinking he had over played his swagger.

A rustling of chairs, the sound of a slap, and a yelp shot through the phone line and burning itself into Henry's mind. He would never forget that moment. Then Sylvia said, "I am here, Henry."

Tommy took the phone back and said, "You bring the book to my warehouse on the south side. You bring it at 11:00 tonight, you come alone.

"I'll be there," Henry said, and hung up the phone.

The wheels were turning; the game was, indeed, on. The next move would be to add one more player to the mix. Henry picked the phone back up and soon had the DA on the phone. Henry masked his disgust and tried to sound upbeat.

"Hey, I have some good news," Henry started.

The DA's voice was calm, "Oh really? What is that?"

"I know you felt terrible about losing the journal. I am a cautious man and I wanted to cover my own ass, so I made a copy before I gave it to you," Henry said, not wanting to anger the DA by telling him that he had been given the copy. Henry was sure the DA would consider that a terrible slight.

"You did?! Well that is fortunate. You must bring it to me immediately," he said, without trying to sound too eager. Henry imagined sweat forming on the DA's brow.

"It is even better. I am meeting Tommy at 11:00 tonight, at his warehouse. You can catch him with the goods."

There was a heavy breath and the DA said, "Yes, that is good. We will get him this time. You have done a great job, Henry. I won't forget this. I'll see you there."

The phone line clicked as the DA hung up. Henry thought to himself, you will certainly remember this night, and that I promise you.

Henry looked at his watch. It was going to be a long wait. He leaned back in his chair and thought about getting a bite to eat. The plan was in motion, but it could go wrong a thousand different ways, even a convicted scum bag on death row gets a last meal.

FORTY NINE

The Forger

The apartment was sparsely decorated, but not because he needed it to be so. It was a choice. The single chair discouraged the rare visitor from lingering. His kitchen consisted of a table, plate, bowl, one set of silverware and two glasses. The second glass he had been given for opening a bank account. It seemed a waste to throw it out, plus he liked the logo design.

Joseph had spent much of his working life travelling the world. His particular skill set took him to every imaginable exotic spot on the globe, at the expense of people who wished to remain anonymous. His extraordinary memory allowed him to sit in his apartment, close his eyes and walk the streets of all of places his life had taken him. Joseph liked to take walks.

If asked, or just if he wanted to, he could describe, in detail, every hotel room in which he had ever stayed. They were much different than his apartment. When on the client's dime, he went first class. Joseph couldn't say if he preferred a five star hotel to his tiny apartment, as he was content in either. It was the feeling of contentment for which he strived each day. Most days he succeeded. If pressed though, he would probably say he preferred to have only what he needed to live.

This is how he viewed his life, as an existence. Joseph didn't feel he was part of the human race, but as a small part of something much bigger. It was his privilege to observe the beauty of the world. And to often copy it, for great reward. Owning a tiny piece of it seemed completely unnecessary. Joseph didn't drink, unless it would be impolite to not do so. Though he didn't care for drink, he loved fine food. His palate was refined. He could discuss flavor and texture with the best chefs in the world and feel right at home.

His phone rang, "Yes, this is me."

"I need you to write a letter. We have samples of the hand writing and what we want it to say."

"When do you need it?"

"I need it now. I realize this isn't how you work, but it is short, and not by a famous hand."

"Send a car to the usual spot. I will be there in 20 minutes."

The apartment was quiet again. He grabbed his set of pens and inks, putting them in his case. Quietly resting in the window was a pleasant little plant. Joseph didn't know what type it was, nor did he especially care. Joseph and the plant seemed to be in agreement about the amount of water and sunlight required, and the plant thrived. He didn't talk to it but liked having the plant in the window. When he was out of town, Mrs. Brumfield would take the plant in. She did talk to it.

He gave the plant some water, before taking the short walk to the meeting place. Normally he would draw each day using either pencil or ink. He would sit in the park and render the fountain or building in exacting detail. His deep focus blocked out the sounds of the frolicking children, but he couldn't keep them from pestering him. Children seemed to be drawn to him, or maybe it was just idle curiosity, but they always asked to see the picture. He would politely show them the drawing. The children would usually say something cute and then run off laughing. To say he didn't care for children would be accurate, but he still felt it was important to be kind.

The corner was three blocks from his house. A black sedan arrived a short time later. Joseph got into the car and was taken to meet the client. He didn't know it, but this wasn't going to be his typical job.

FIFTY

Two Hours To Go

The evening air was chilly. It was above freezing, so everything was wet. An odor of damp and despair, swirled about. Henry parked his car a couple of blocks from the warehouse. He was two hours early. Henry calculated that the number of outcomes, which ended with him floating face down in the East River, as being considerably greater than the number where he slept in his own bed.

With this fuzzy and upsetting math in his head, he decided it would be best to look over the property, check for all the routes of egress, and generally get a feel for the place. Henry had been in tight spots before, some which nearly ended in sorrow, but because he was good at seeing the options and reading his adversary, he had gotten through unscathed.

The warehouse was in a part of town, which was teeming with life during the day, as ships brought in goods, and the trucks took them away. When 5:00 pm arrived, everything ground to a halt. There would be about 30 minutes of chaos, as everyone scurried off to their lives, and then it would be quiet.

The city is never completely quiet though. Henry listened to the city sounds, as he walked slowly around the blocks adjacent to the warehouse property. He checked doors, which might be unlocked. He looked for escape routes, which might lead them into a dead end, both literally and figuratively. He covered all the angles, as they say.

Henry had a plan A and a plan B. Running away from Tommy and his thugs on foot, with a frightened, likely exhausted Sylvia, was plan Q. But one never knows; it is best to try to think of everything. There were a bunch of variables and he counted on a lot of egos in the room. There would be more guns than Henry could imagine. He had his own revolver. It would likely be futile to try to shoot his way out of a jam, but he added it to the plan list, somewhere around letter M.

The far side of the warehouse was next to the river. The docks had a few sailors meandering about, smoking, securing lines, and a bum on a bench drinking a bottle of wine out of a bag. Henry chuckled to himself. He wondered if the bum would agree that 'Gallo Brings You Fine Wine'. He shook his head from side to side and brought his focus back to Sylvia.

Henry moved in to take a closer look at the warehouse. He didn't think she was here yet, as he imagined Tommy was planning on bringing her here shortly before their meeting. Of course, Tommy wasn't known for thinking things through, perhaps they had been here all day? The windows were filthy and at first look, all of them on the ground level, were impossible to see through.

Henry decided it was too risky to try one of the doors. Looking around for another way to see inside, he saw a promising spot. Near one end there was a stack of pallets, which were in front of a window and they had pushed out one of the panes of glass. He carefully removed the pallets from the stack, one by one, and then looked through the hole. He couldn't see the entire warehouse, but he could listen, and there weren't any sounds. It was still.

He looked at his pocket watch, one hour had slipped by, and now he was as ready as he could be. Henry began to fidget. The tension was getting almost unbearable and he needed to be calm, with a clear head. He walked down a street, which seemed like it might have a bar.

The sign said, "Joe's Place"; there was an ad for Lucky Strikes in the window. Henry didn't smoke much, but he needed one now. The bartender was wiping the bar with an ancient artifact of a bar towel, and grunted, "What can I get ya, Mack?"

"Pack of Luckys," Henry said, leaving off the please, as he figured such a politeness might come off as being a wise guy. Henry's brain was firing on all cylinders. Just the idea that he would worry about a 'please', and how it might change the dynamic, told him he was ready. The meeting would be tense and the slightest blunder could be deadly. The bartender set a fresh pack on the counter; Henry paid him, grabbed a book of matches, and gave a quick look around the bar.

Henry wasn't sure who he was looking for. But there is a point, when facing a possible end, which makes one look for the familiar, the friendly. There was nothing familiar or friendly about this crowd. Henry gave a clipped, "Thanks", and walked out.

He tapped the Luckys several times, opened it, and pulled a cigarette from the pack. The first match didn't light, but the second did the trick. He walked back to his car. The coolness of the evening, the dampness of the air, and the glow of the cigarette in hand seemed exactly as it should be.

Now Henry felt the calmness and clarity, which he knew he needed. Forty eight minutes until the meet.

Fifty One

Three Minutes Before Midnight

Henry stood outside the warehouse; it was 3 minutes before midnight. The door on the right side, near the first loading bay, opened up and a thick man in an overcoat motioned him forward.

It was probably only 25 yards from where Henry had parked his car, but the walk seemed tiring. Sal held the door for Henry, in a very non-threatening way. He didn't snarl or make any comment, he just said, "This way, Mr. Wood." His politeness seemed out of place. Sal towered over Henry. Henry guessed that he must be 6' 8."

Sal walked behind Henry, directing him past a stack of crates and towards the large open area in the center of the warehouse. There were two sedans parked there, and when Henry appeared with Sal, the doors opened up and several men emerged. Two of them held Tommy guns, one had a sawed off shotgun, and two more had pistols. They didn't raise the guns, but it was apparent they were ready for any 'tricks'.

Henry stopped about 15 feet from the front of the two sedans. Sal walked over and opened the back door on the one to the right. Out stepped Sylvia and then Tommy 'The Knife', with his arm around her waist. She had a frightened and disgusted look on her face. Henry stayed stoic.

"You got quite a girl here, Henry, she is a looker," Tommy said as he gave her a squeeze. He was trying to get a reaction out of Henry. He failed.

"You doing alright, Sylvia?"

"Yes," said Sylvia in a tired voice.

"You have caused me a lot of problems, Mr. Wood; you and your journal."

"It isn't my journal. I am just holding it for a friend."

"I know all about the Journal, and that scum, pencil pushing accountant Alexander, who wrote about stuff that wasn't any of his concern." Tommy's voice flashed into angry, which Henry assumed was his normal tone. "I also know how this little chickadee's father helped him."

"Oh you do, do you? You are so clever. What else can you tell me?" Henry said, stalling for time.

"You want a story, tough guy?" Tommy said, smugly. "I bet you think that the cavalry is about to show up and save the day? I have a story for you, they ain't coming."

Just then a door behind Henry opened and a man walked through alone. Henry turned around for a look. It was the DA. Tommy laughed a deep hearty laugh as Mark walked up and stood next to Henry.

"I stand corrected, here is your cavalry."

Henry looked at the DA and wasn't sure how the next few minutes would play out, so he decided to play his part. "You came alone?"

More laughter from Tommy and then, "He didn't come alone; he is here with his friends. It's just that you aren't one of them." He gave the DA a nod and Mark McKinley reached over and patted Henry down until he felt the journal. He took it and walked over and handed it to Tommy; then turned to Henry, "You couldn't leave well enough alone?"

"You dirty rat. I can't believe you are in Tommy's pocket. You disgust me," Henry said, feigning surprise.

Tommy felt like a bit of gloating, so he pushed Sylvia towards Henry and said, "Here is your little chickadee. A deal is a deal."

Henry could tell it wasn't over yet.

"The problem is, well, you know my secret, Henry. The cavalry is on the payroll, which means we have a problem. As I see it, you and your little friend, know too much."

Sal looked at Sylvia. He knew this moment would arrive and just assumed he would do as he was told. She looked back at him, holding Henry's arm, looking frightened for both of them. There was something else in her eyes. She looked at him with hope. Sal was facing a dilemma and knew that the decision he made next would change his life.

There was the faintest sound from outside. Tommy didn't notice, but Henry did. Since plan A was out the window, Henry moved on to plan B. "You have your journal, there isn't any more evidence. My job is done. Why don't you just let the girl go, and we can discuss my keeping your secret."

Tommy laughed, "Trying to negotiate Henry? From a very weak position, I might add."

"You don't want to kill us, that would be messy, and..."

"Messy! Oh it will be messy. You've caused me all sorts of pain. I've lost good men. I'm going to relish watching you suffer, you little prick. You don't have any idea what is about to happen to you."

The sounds from outside, the faint scuffling of feet, stopped and Henry said, "I have some idea what is about to happen." A smile worked its way across Henry's face.

Tommy was standing just a few feet away from Henry and saw the smile. He didn't understand.

Four of the dock bays opened up simultaneously. The relative calm of the warehouse was broken by several hundred men with guns, walking in four groups towards the little meeting. Tommy's boys instinctively drew their weapons. The look on their faces was a mixture of confusion and fear.

The four groups walked in and positioned themselves around the meeting. The top guns from each of the other four families now stood with deafening silence around Tommy, his men, and Henry and Sylvia. The heads of each of the four families walked through the open bays. They eased their way toward the front, with their personal guards by their sides. A man from each group found a chair and placed it in front of the their respective bosses.

Tommy's voice was unsteady. "Frankie, what brings you out tonight?"

Frankie was the top boss. He had been running the streets of NY for over 40 years, and it was because of the respect and fear, which he commanded, that the squabbles between the families never got out of hand. In his 70's, he was still in fantastic shape. The other family heads were considerably more portly but were not to be taken lightly.

Frankie took off his topcoat and handed it to one of his men. He removed a cigar and lighter. Biting off the end, he slowly rolled the cigar in the flame until it was lit. Once lit, Frankie sat down in the chair, which was about 5 feet to Henry's right. The other bosses took their seats.

Henry snuck a peak at the DA, who looked terrified. His eyes were wide and it seemed like he might have stopped breathing.

Frankie took a few puffs from his cigar and spoke. "It is awfully late to be doing business down here at the docks,

Tommy?" The question was rhetorical, so Tommy just nodded.

"Speak up, Tommy, my boy, what are you doing here in the middle of the night?"

"Just cleaning up some loose ends, Frankie, nothing you need to worry about."

"I see the district attorney, Mr. Mark McKinley, is joining us." Frankie gave a nod to the DA, who managed a feeble smile. "Tommy hasn't broken any laws now has he?"

Sylvia, who didn't know who these men were and had no idea what was going on, "That scum bag kidnapped me, and the DA is in it with him. He is a ..." Henry grabbed her arm and gave it a squeeze. She stopped talking, realizing that Henry seemed to have a plan.

Frankie stood up slowly and turned towards Sylvia, "He did? Well, that isn't right." He looked at Tommy, "She is such a lovely young woman." He took her hand and patted the back of it. Frankie had grandkids, and the oldest was a spitfire. Sylvia reminded him of her. "Tommy, why did you take this young woman?"

"Her father was sticking his nose in our business," Tommy said, with a bit too much swagger.

Frankie let go of Sylvia's hand and walked up to Tommy. "He wasn't sticking it in our business; he was sticking it in your business!"

Tommy didn't say anything.

"What we have here is a management issue," Frankie said calmly, walking around Tommy in a circle. The other bosses nodded and made little noises of agreement. "You made your bones, Tommy, and we rewarded you. But you have not been a good boss. Perhaps it is your youth? But there are rules which we don't break."

He blew a ring of smoke over Tommy's head. Tommy stood silently. Henry doubted Tommy could have moved, even if he'd wanted to. Frankie continued, "Rule 1: We don't use the children, especially the daughters of our enemies, to handle our business." His voice was getting louder. "Rule 2: We don't discuss family business with accountants or lawyers!"

Sylvia took Henry's hand and crept in behind him. Henry gave it a squeeze. She looked at Sal, who was staring at Tommy. Sal seemed relaxed, or maybe he agreed, she didn't know.

"Rule 3: There are certain people we don't mess with. Big Mike is one of those people. He may be a cop, but he is a straight shooter, and he's from the neighborhood."

Big Mike was well liked by everyone, even the bad guys, and Tommy had stepped over the line when they beat him, beat him nearly to death. Henry had hoped that Mike could talk to Frankie and persuade him to intervene. When Mike called, he didn't even need to ask.

There was some shifting about. Tommy's guys had lowered their guns, and all but Sal were moving slowly away. A guy in a grey overcoat and hat, which was pulled below his eyes, now stood behind DA, Mark McKinley.

Frankie stopped speaking and made a gesture to one of the other bosses. He stood up and waved towards the back of his group of men. A small man in a dark suit, who wore very thick glasses, stepped forward. He carried a briefcase.

The small man whispered something to Frankie. Frankie smiled, and then the small man opened his briefcase and removed a single piece of paper. He held it in front of Frankie to read. The small man wore cotton gloves and held the piece of paper as if it were a treasure.

Frankie looked at one of his lieutenants, and several men stepped forward to relieve all of Tommy's men of their firearms. He then took a revolver and Tommy's prized hunting knife, which he had bought shortly after he earned his moniker. The lieutenant handed it to Frankie. After admiring the blade for a really long moment, Frankie said, while waving his hand in front of him, "We have discussed how you are handling your affairs. It appears to the other distinguished family heads, that you lack certain management skills, which are necessary." The other bosses nodded, one of them spit on the ground.

Tommy was trying to keep his cool, "This whole journal mess is behind us. I was about to take care of the last of the loose ends, before you interrupted...er...joined us." Tommy had gone too far. Frankie shook the knife at Tommy, "Interrupted! I am sorry to hear that you feel a visit from the other families is such an inconvenience." Tommy stammered, but Frankie wouldn't let him interrupt. "This is just another example of your incompetence." Then he lowered his tone and walked a few paces away from Tommy.

Tommy didn't say a word. Frankie continued, "But I am nothing if not a fair man. Let's ask some of your men what they think about your management skills. Who wants to go first?" There was silence for about two seconds, just long enough that Tommy thought his men were going to stand by him, but then his own first lieutenant spoke.

At 6' 8", Sal's voice was as deep as one would expect, but his tone and eloquence startled everyone. "He is a horrific leader. He lets his considerable temper affect his decisions, often resulting in lost opportunities, difficult situations, and generally causing the family financial distress." Tommy looked both surprised and angry. His other men all turned towards Sal with blank expressions of disbelief. If one were to ask his men, it is unlikely that any had heard him say much more than "yes boss" or "get to it." The murmuring from the several hundred men with guns was considerable and lasted until Frankie spoke again.

Frankie couldn't remember a time in his life when he liked being surprised. He associated it with bad things. This time, however, he was both surprised and pleased. Were he alone, he would have smiled broadly. He was not alone and said, "Hypothetically, if there were to become an opening in one of our operations, might you be interested in..." he paused for effect, "...being considered for the position?"

Sal responded in a more expected manner with a simple, "Yes."

Tommy was starting to sweat.

Frankie leaned in to whisper something to Sal, who then stepped over to Tommy, removed his money belt and handed it to Frankie. It had exactly $50,000 in hundred dollar bills, made up of 5 neat stacks. Frankie had come to the meeting with a plan, which all the other bosses had agreed was the best way to handle things. Now he had an idea, and he gathered the other bosses together for a quiet chat. There was nodding among the bosses, though nobody could hear what was being said. They each returned to their chairs. Some of them lit their own cigars.

When Frankie returned to his spot, he noticed Sylvia, who was looking rather disheveled from her experience. "Where are my manners? You must feel awful after your terrible experience. Henry, why don't you take the young lady home? We have things under control." Then he took her hand, kissed it gently, and said, "You and your friends will not be bothered by Tommy any more. You have my word on that."

Sylvia smiled, "Thank you", and then she whispered so only Frankie could hear. "Sal was very nice to me. He brought me food and kept me company. He was a gentleman." Frankie smiled this time and leaned in and whispered something to her. Sylvia grabbed Henry's hand. Sal was looking at her and she flashed a quick smile.

Henry didn't like the mob. He didn't like criminals in general, but sometimes it is hard to tell the good guys from the bad, and this was one of those times. He wasn't sure where he stood with Frankie, what the account balance would be, but for now, Sylvia was safe. He put his arm around her shoulder and walked her out of the warehouse. As he reached the door, Henry let Sylvia go first, and he stole a quick glance. The little man was holding the document which he had shown Frankie, in front of the DA's face, which was now ashen.

Henry thought he knew what was going on, but even if he were wrong, the loose ends were being tended to by the men with their cigars and guns. He would make some calls, read the paper and use his contacts to verify his suspicions tomorrow. Tonight he would tend to Sylvia and look in on Luna.

FIFTY TWO

New Boss

When the door closed, Frankie handed the entire 50K to Sal. "We've decided to give you a tryout, as it were. Tommy has become a problem, as has the DA. I'm not promising to give you the entire city if you pass. I am giving you on opportunity to demonstrate judgment and management skills. Your first test will be to deal with this problem. Hire your team, do what you think is best. Were it me, I would make it a long slow process, but I leave it up to you."

Sal was ready. He had thought about this day, but didn't imagine it coming so soon. He could remember every decision he had disagreed with, every insult he had endured, and all the blunders Tommy had made. He looked at Frankie and then walked over to the group of men who, up until a few minutes ago, had worked for Tommy. He didn't say a word but peeled off a thousand dollars and handed it to each one. When he got to the last man, his driver, he gave him five thousand, and said, "You just got promoted. We'll talk about it later."

"Yes, boss."

Tommy had been pushed past the limits of reason and started yelling, "You filthy back stabbing bastard. I will..."

Sal spun around and with a massive backhand, cracked him across the face, breaking Tommy's jaw. He crumpled to the ground. Sal said, "Put him in the car. Don't be gentle...gentlemen."

Frankie liked what he saw. The other bosses did too, though Anthony was starting to fume over not getting Manhattan, but he knew better than to bring it up now. Sal walked over to each boss and took each of them by the hand, kissed their rings, and thanked them. When he got to Anthony, he towered over him. Despite this, he still looked humble. He kissed Anthony's ring, then leaned in and whispered, "I know my history. I know about your father and what happened with Manhattan. If I pass my test, and you will allow it, I would like to discuss how we can right this injustice."

Nobody could hear what he had said, but the look on Anthony's face told them he had won him over. Sal walked back to the center of the room and kissed Frankie's ring. "Thank you for this opportunity. May I make a small request?"

Frankie liked his respect, though he thought it a little cheeky to be asking favors already, but he wanted to hear what it was, so he said, "Tell me what you need."

"May I have his knife, to help in the solving of the situation?"

Frankie roared. "Get a load of this one," he turned around and everyone was laughing, well, except Mark McKinley. "You got style Salvatore." He handed him the knife.

Sal walked over to the small man in the suit. The man opened the letter so he could read it. Sal was smart enough not to touch. The letter was returned to the envelope and put inside another one. All he said to Sal, when he handed it to him, "No finger prints." Sal carefully tucked it into his pocket and then, using the knife, tapped the DA on the shoulder. "Get in the car."

FIFTY THREE

Reunion

Sylvia was homeless, overwrought over the loss of Winston, and more exhausted than she had ever been. Henry put her up in the hotel next to his office. He promised her he would come back and watch over her, but he had to let Mike and Luna know they were all right. He left her crying into a pillow.

Though he, too, was beat, he was anxious to get Mike on the phone. Henry briskly walked up the stairs, and when he entered the hallway, there was Bobby standing there. "Is Sylvia ok?" he asked.

Henry didn't know how Bobby knew what was going on, but he was too tired to inquire, so he said, "Yes, she is just fine. Thanks." Henry noticed that Bobby looked really tired, too. *Had he been worrying?* "How are you holding up, buddy?"

Bobby's eyes flashed when he heard the word 'buddy'. He was so touched that Henry had shown concern; he was momentarily at a loss. It was a very brief moment. "I am great now! I was worried about how things were going. Too bad about Winston, he was a great guy. But it looks like the good guys came out on top, in this one."

Henry smiled, "Yep, I guess you are right. Now, if da bums could just beat the Yankees this year."

Bobby shook his head, "I think they got a good chance this year." Then he winked.

Henry couldn't help but chuckle at this strange little man. He patted him on the shoulder and wandered down the hall to his office. He heard Bobby go back into his office.

Henry picked up the phone and dialed Mike. It rang just once. "Hey, Henry, that you?"

"Yep, it's me." Henry heard Luna in the background. "Tell Luna we are fine."

After Mike relayed the message, he said, "So how did it go down?"

"It worked just like you thought. Your old pal Frankie showed up with an army. All the bosses were there, and Tommy nearly wet himself."

"Did McKinley show?"

"Ya, he was there. Didn't look so good when I left, though. A small man with thick glasses showed him some piece of paper. I didn't know what it was about, but figured it was something you and Frankie cooked up."

"When I talked with Frankie, I mentioned the problem, told him the whole story, but I didn't 'cook' anything up. I am a cop you know. I can't be a party to anything Frankie might decide to do. That being said, I think I know who the guy was."

"It sounds like Mikeyangelo; sort of a play on his middle name, Michael and Michelangelo. I think his first name is Joseph. He is a forger; probably the best forger this side of Sicily."

"So what was on the paper?" Henry asked.

"I have no idea, but I would bet it will show up as evidence. Again, I 'officially' know nothing. But I do know how Frankie's mind works. If I had one guess, it is probably some sort of suicide note, or something about Tommy, a 'Should I Show Up Dead' sort of letter.'

They talked for a few more minutes. Henry gave an account of what he imagined was happening to Tommy. They finished by Mike agreeing to make sure Luna gets down to the office in the morning. He hadn't been there yet, but she knew where it was, so he would have her drive.

Henry went back to the hotel room and sacked out in the chair. Sylvia was fast asleep.

Fifty Four

Meeting With The Captain

Henry sat in the captain's office. They were waiting for Mike, and the silence was a little bit disconcerting. Henry tried to focus on anything but the question he was about to be asked. There were different answers he could give, all of them with portions of truth, but none explaining things fully.

Henry liked black and white. He thought of himself as being on the side of the law, but now, well it was a grey area. If there had been another way, he would have jumped at it. He didn't have regrets, but he did have misgivings about what he would say to the captain.

Mike knocked and entered. He took the chair next to Henry.

The captain said, "I appreciate the two of you coming in today, especially you, Mike, considering. How's the arm?"

"Getting better by the day."

"Good to hear it." He paused and looked at some papers on the desk. It was apparent that he was choosing his words carefully. "We are closing a few cases. It seems that our DA was a crook, or at least, that is what his suicide note said."

Henry considered looking surprised, but thought better of it. Mike didn't move. "There have been a few upstanding citizens who have come forward with all sorts of details about the gang war killings. It seems the recently departed

Tommy 'The Knife' ordered many of the hits. We have no reason to believe otherwise, except..."

The word hung there until Henry said, "Except, captain?"

"Except that the first shots were fired at Tommy, so we don't know who started the war." He looked at Henry. "You have any ideas, which you would be eager to share?"

Henry suppressed his smile. The captain had, indeed, chosen his words with care and he answered, "I can say with complete honesty that there isn't anything I am eager to add."

The captain looked at Mike but didn't say anything. Mike decided the question was for him too, "Me either, captain." The captain looked relieved, slapped his hands on his desk. "Good then. I guess a few of these will end up in the cold files. I can live with that. Thanks for coming in."

Mike and Henry stood up and shook the captain's hand. As they were leaving, "Hey boys, let's just keep the details of our official discussion, well..."

"I'm not saying a thing." Henry said. Mike nodded. The captain returned to his desk.

Mike and Henry said goodbye, deciding to try to have lunch in a week or so. Mike suggested they invite Francis. Henry didn't understand, but was glad they were finally friends, and that was good.

FIFTY FIVE

Recap at Flatiron

When Henry and Sylvia walked into the Flatiron building, Mike and Luna were waiting. Henry gave a recap of the events for Luna's sake, though she had already heard most of it from Mike. They were joined by Bobby, who wanted to hear the story. So Henry told it again.

The relief on the faces of both ladies was easy to spot, but it quickly changed to glee, when their fathers knocked on the door. The stories were told again. Luna and her father insisted that Sylvia and her father stay with them, while they deal with their burned out house. Henry never had a chance to ask about how they got him the clues, or learned that it was ok to come out of hiding.

Three days later, Winston was laid to rest.

The body of DA Mark McKinley had been found. When the police searched his home, they found a folio with a hand written letter from the DA, explaining all of the work he had done for Tommy, and how he expected that his life might be in danger. An anonymous concerned citizen had left a message that the man who stabbed the DA to death, could be found near the docks. Tommy was badly beaten; both eyes were swollen shut, his tongue had been cut out. He was tied to a crate of rotting fish. Though his arm was still in a sling, Big Mike was in uniform and read Tommy his rights.

The papers all guessed, correctly, that Tommy had gone over the line with the DA. Nobody ever questioned the letter or how the stabbing was done, it was an open and shut case. What they didn't know was that it was the carelessness with which he had used the DA, and that it was because he had beaten an old friend of Frankie's, which had led to his demise.

Henry was paid for the case and thanked profusely. Luna left him a bonus plate of cookies, and a promise to make more, whenever he wanted. Sylvia brought in a few plants for his office and hired someone to do a lovely stencil over his door. "Henry Wood Detective Agency"

Bobby stopped in to let Henry know that his old phone number had now been transferred to his new phone. The first call was from his old office neighbor, Francis, who invited him for lunch, on the paper.

FIFTY SIX

Henry, Mr. Culberson, and Mr. Alexander

Henry, Mr. Culberson and Mr. Alexander, gathered at a diner, it was 5 am and most of the morning crowd hadn't arrived yet. They had been up all night, celebrating their reunion with their daughters and the end of the nightmare of the previous few weeks. Henry still had a few questions.

"What I am having trouble wrapping my head around, is how you found me and knew I would be up to it."

Mr. Alexander, "We had been worried for most of December and finally Mr. Culberson said we needed a plan, in case we were discovered."

Mr. Culberson, "Which we were. I was busy coding the information which had been found, when he called me and said someone had been through his office."

Henry, "Who?"

Mr. Alexander, "I don't know, somebody at the firm, I suspect, but I have no idea. As you figured out, I am meticulous and the journal was always kept hidden. But I made a mistake, when I overheard a couple of the lawyers discussing some work they were doing for Tommy. I went back to my office and quickly wrote down all the details, though I didn't include names, and put the piece of paper in my right desk drawer, under three files, and placed a tiny pencil sharpener near the bottom right, such that it was approximately one inch from each edge of the corner."

Henry, "And if the sharpener was moved, you would know someone had opened the drawer?"

"Yes."

"But isn't it possible someone could just be looking for a pencil or something? Couldn't it have been completely innocent?"

"Oh yes, it is rare, but sometimes my secretary will put something away, or look for a file. On this occasion though, she was with me, taking dictation for the interview with a new client. We were in the meeting for two hours and the first thing I did upon returning was to get ready to head home. When I opened the drawer, careful not to do it too quickly, and thus, move my marker. I noticed it was gone."

"Gone?"

"Well it turns out someone had gone through the drawer, lifting up the files and finding my paper underneath. They refolded it and returned everything, but the sharpener. It was in the back of the drawer, under the files."

Mr. Culberson, "He called me immediately and was rather frantic. I told him to tell me what they had seen and he read me the notes. The notes were very general and didn't mention Tommy at all, so I calmed him down and we decided to meet to discuss our next move."

Their food arrived. Henry had a patty melt and fries and listened intently to them tell their tale. "What was your next move?" he asked while salting the fries.

Mr. Culberson took a bite of pancakes and chewed it slowly, while Mr. Alexander smiled, knowing he wanted to tell the next part, because it was his idea.

Mr. Culberson, "I was worried about the safety of our daughters and from the beginning I had been contemplating this day arriving. Winston knew a little bit about the plans and I told him our next move. We blew up the lab and I went into hiding."

Henry, "Why didn't you tell your daughters?"

"They are both strong willed women and well, we were worried about telling them. Their safety came first and we agreed that if they knew, they would be in far greater danger. I made Winston promise not to tell Sylvia anything and I went to a hotel. I had plenty of cash and moved every day for a week and then decided it was best to get out of the city."

"Where did you go?" Henry was on the edge of his seat.

"I ended up taking the train to DC. I met a man who had a place for rent and he travelled back and forth a couple of times per week. He was very helpful in our plans." He looked at Mr. Culberson.

"So you were still going to work?" Henry was amazed.

"Yes, every day while we figured out our next move."

"What was that?"

"We needed someone to entrust with the journal. But we needed to know they were smart and honest."

"Is that why you kept the codex and journal separate?"

"Yes."

Henry finished his fries and started to work on his patty melt.

Mr. Alexander, "The first clue was my idea. I reasoned that if you found it, and made it to the address where we hid the journal, you were clever."

Henry, "But what if someone had bought the cabinet before I had found it?"

Mr. Culberson, "Somebody did buy it. Me. I purchased it, paid cash and gave them an extra hundred to hold on to it. I told them I was going to be out of town."

Henry, "So how did you pick me?"

They looked at each other, with sort of blank expressions. "It was fate. I just happened into a guy in a bar one night, and he was telling the bartender about this great detective who had helped him out. I asked him who it was; he fumbled through his pockets and dug out your card."

"Was that the card Sylvia gave me?"

Henry couldn't stand it anymore; he had to ask the one question, which had been bothering him more than any other. "How does the closet work?"

They both looked at each other. Mr. Alexander, "What closet?"

"Where you sent the stuff?" Henry didn't say from the future, as there were people in the booth next to them.

"Which stuff?"

"The books and the DVD."

Neither man knew what to say. Finally Mr. Alexander said, "What's a DVD?"

Henry could tell they were being genuine. He had assumed the explosion had been part of some sort of time travel experiment. His guess was that Mr. Culberson had been hiding out in the future, but now those theories all seemed to evaporate. He decided to brush off the question, "How did you get the clues to me?"

Mr. Alexander, "I did the pencils before I went into hiding with Mr. Culberson."

Mr. Culberson, "The clever bit in my library, well I had Winston take care of that for me, with instructions not to help you find it. I wanted to be sure you were as clever as we had hoped."

Mr. Alexander, "The clue we had hidden at MOMA, well that was a very clever one. I decided it was worth the risk to come back into town..."

Henry asked, "The clue at MOMA, what clue at MOMA?"

Mr. Culberson, looking disappointed, "You didn't find the instructions, behind the bear display in the gift shop?"

"No. What are you talking about?"

Now everyone was confused. Mr. Alexander, "I gave specific instructions about where to hide the clues." Now both Mr. Alexander and Mr. Culberson were arguing about clue placement and that they shouldn't have trusted the guy from DC. They were both getting very upset until Henry pointed out that he had figured it out anyway. This seemed to satisfy them and Henry was glad they didn't ask how he had done it.

They finished their food and went their separate ways. Henry was tired, too tired to worry about how the closet worked or who had sent him the clues. If the person or persons wanted him to know, they would tell him. Maybe he would just have to wait until he got to the future to find out.

Made in the USA
Charleston, SC
25 July 2011